HIGHLAND KNIGHT OF DREAMS

AMY JARECKI

All rights reserved.

No part of this publication may be sold, copied, distributed, reproduced or transmitted in any form or by any means, mechanical or digital, including photocopying and recording or by any information storage and retrieval system without the prior written permission of both the publisher, Oliver Heber Books and the author, Amy Jarecki, except in the case of brief quotations embodied in critical articles and reviews.

PUBLISHER'S NOTE: This is a work of fiction. Names, characters, places, and incidents either are the product of the author's imagination or are used fictitiously. Any resemblance to actual persons, living or dead, business establishments, events, or locales is entirely coincidental.

Copyright © 2019 by Amy Jarecki

Published by Oliver-Heber Books

0 9 8 7 6 5 4 3 2 1

Chapter One

THE HIGHLANDS OF SCOTLAND, 1670

"Did you see her?" Quinn's gaze darted through the forest, honing like a falcon as he searched for the beauty. With a dig of his spurs, he cantered ahead, leaving his companions in his wake.

"Her? Are ye seeing selkies now, brother?" hollered Eachan, his horse losing speed behind.

Glenn MacGregor's grandiose laugh resounded like cannon fire, the warrior's mount nearly able to keep pace. "Quinn most likely saw a rabbit. No matter, I'm hungry and up for the chase."

Certain his eyes hadn't deceived him, Quinn lurched over his horse's withers, demanding a gallop. "Haste, ye beast!" He scanned the foliage for any flicker of movement, for a glimpse of a blue gown. No, he hadn't seen a vision. He'd seen a goddess.

To where had she disappeared? As plain as the nose on his face he'd spotted her standing in a clearing. The sun's rays illuminated wisps of her waist-length hair as it glittered like gold. The wind set her skirts to sail, and they billowed in a surreal whirlwind of color.

For the briefest of moments she'd stood like a doe, her eyes wide, her stance majestic, yet sensing impending danger. When the nymph had spotted him, she'd turned and fled as if she thought Quinn the devil incarnate.

With a slight twist of his reins, he steered his horse inland and through the trees. Above, a ruined castle loomed over an outcropping.

Is that where you're hiding, beauty?

Giving another tap of his heels, horse and rider ascended the hill. At the summit, he hopped down and ran up a set of unsteady barbican steps, taking two at a time. Nearly toppling to his death as old mortar crumbled beneath his feet, he caught himself on a merlon. A stone dropped from the side of the wall, thundering as it tumbled down the sheer slope overlooking the Firth of Clyde. Without a flinch, Quinn scanned the grounds and turned full circle.

"Ballocks!"

"Lost her, did ye?" shouted Eachan, who hadn't yet dismounted.

MacGregor joined Quinn atop the unstable masonry—the henchman was rather nimble for a beast. "Must have been a selkie, sent from the waters to drive you mad."

At six-feet, Quinn was formidable in any man's eyes though he had to crane his neck to meet Glenn's gaze. "She wasn't a bloody creature. I ken what I saw."

His friend gave a shrug. "I'm only disappointed it wasn't a rabbit. I'm weary of dried mutton and oatcakes."

"Stop your bellyaching," Quinn said as he continued to watch for movement. "We've only been riding for a day."

"Doesn't matter." MacGregor slapped his belly. "I'd welcome a rabbit or three cooked over an open fire."

"Aye? Mayhap you'll find one whilst we make camp."

"Here?" asked Eachan, still sitting his mount.

"Why not?" After taking one last scan of the forest,

Quinn climbed back down to what must have been the courtyard of a medieval fortress.

"These are the ruins of Toward Castle, that's why," said his brother, ever the wary one.

MacGregor grunted behind. "Lamont lands."

"Campbell lands now," said Quinn. "The Lamonts are long gone, and the crumbling keep beneath our feet is owned by our father."

Eachan peered over his shoulder as if he expected to be set upon at any moment. "Do not say that too loudly."

"Why? The selkies will hear us?" Quinn thrust his finger up the barbican wall. "I was just up there with a view that rivals Stirling Castle's wall-walk and there's nary a soul for miles."

"Aside from the beauty you thought you sighted," said MacGregor.

"Wheesht." Quinn gave his friend's arm a thwack. "I ken what I saw."

Eachan finally dismounted. "Are you certain it was a woman? Last time you chased after a lass she ended up having a beard."

"Aye, and you're full of vinegar." Perhaps he'd imagined the woman—God knew he hadn't enjoyed company of the feminine variety in ages, something he hoped to rectify come the fête at Rothesay Castle. Regardless, the lovely was long gone and he'd never see her again.

Blast.

Quinn set to removing his mount's saddle and hobbling the horse's front legs. "MacGregor, since you have a taste for rabbits, why not go fetch us a few? Eachan and I will tend to making camp for the night."

"I am at your command, Your Lordship." God's blood, the man liked to poke fun.

Just because Quinn was the firstborn son of an earl, didn't

mean he was one to shirk common duties. Being a laggard nobleman might work in England, but idleness had no place in the Highlands. "Would you rather I hunt?"

"Nay." Heading for his horse, MacGregor pulled his musket from its scabbard. "With all these trees about, it will be easy enough to find a warren—or a deer. I'll return in the hour."

"Good," said Eachan. "All this talk about food is making my stomach growl."

"When isn't it?" Quinn set to work, tossing boulders aside to clear a place to sleep. "Go on and start a fire. Mayhap it will keep your selkies at bay whilst we sleep."

"They're not my bloody selkies. You're the one who's seeing things."

Quinn straightened and thumped his chest. "Women, mind you. I can spot a bonny lass from miles away."

"And you're full of shite."

"Possibly, but if so, you'll be eating it for the rest of your days."

"Brothers. Why God saw to make me the second son, I'll never understand," Eachan mumbled as he wandered toward the trees. He stooped and picked up a stick of wood. "Ye ken this place is haunted."

"Now do not tell me you're afraid of a wee ghost." Quinn chuckled, kicking away the smaller pebbles. "God's blood, you were just teasing me about seeing selkies. Mayhap 'tis you whose head is full of fantastical delusions."

He switched tack and began stacking the boulders in a circular fire pit. The stones had fallen from the castle walls—a fortress he was well aware had been razed by his grandfather, the Earl of Argyll, a bloodthirsty zealot. It was oft difficult to admit he had descended from such a man's loins. Grandad had nearly ruined the Campbell legacy, so much so, the tyrant had been beheaded as a traitor in Edinburgh's

Grassmarket Square—a humiliation the family desperately wanted to forget.

·❧·

ALICE PUSHED THROUGH THE DOOR OF THE THATCHED-ROOF cottage. "Gran!" she shouted, pressing her hand against her chest as she gulped in deep breaths of air.

When she didn't find her grandmother sitting in the rocking chair by the hearth, she yelled again, "Gran!"

The only parent Alice had ever known came hobbling out of the bedchamber carrying her cane rather than using it. "What is it, lass? You're shouting so loudly, they'll be able to hear you clear across the Clyde."

She'd run nearly two miles and was in sore need of a drink of water. "F-forgive me, but you'll never believe who I saw."

"After five and seventy years, you'd be surprised what I'd believe." Gran made an exaggerated show at looking from one of Alice's hands to the other. "Where is your basket?"

"Who cares about the basket?" Patting her chest, Alice dashed for the ewer sitting on the table and poured herself a drink.

"You're panting." Limping nearer, Gran shook her cane. "Have you been running?"

"Aye, near two miles." Alice guzzled the contents of the wooden cup. "But you must listen to—"

"Heaven's child. Sit down and calm yourself."

Ready to jump out of her skin, the last thing Alice wanted to do was sit. But after meeting her grandmother's indignant stare, she inhaled deeply, made herself calm down and sat on the bench. "I was searching for yarrow in the wood when the ground rumbled with the pounding of horse hooves."

"Do not tell me King William has sent an army."

"It sounded like an army, but it was three knights—three Campbell men."

"Campbells?" Gran's expression grew dark before she turned to the hob and used a ladle to stir the pottage. "What made you think they are knights?"

"They were armed like knights—swords, muskets, dirks and targes. And they were carrying the Earl of Argyll's pennant."

Gran spat, whipping back around. "Argyll?" She clutched the ladle over her heart and squeezed, her face turning white as bed linens. "God forbid that name be uttered in this house."

"Forgive me—I ken they're evil. Worse, they're making camp at Toward Castle."

The old woman's face grew so dark, it was as if a raincloud had come into the cottage, threatening to drench them both.

And Alice knew why. Moreover, she wanted to do whatever she could to face these men and make them pay for the heinous crimes committed four and twenty years ago—the year of her birth. "I can take a vial of poison and spill it into the burn. No one will ken it was me."

"Poison?" Gran exchanged the ladle for her cane while a flash of ire sparked in her deep blue eyes. Though the elderly woman's face had grown as withered as a prune, her eyes still gleamed with astute discerning. "Alice, do you have any idea what those brigands would do to you if you were discovered?"

"Ye ken I will not be. I'm as stealthy as a ghost—learned from the best of ghosts." She grinned, flapping her eyelashes at the woman who'd been her tutor.

"Nay, 'tis too much of a risk. Besides, what if you ended up killing an innocent?"

Gran paced for a moment, stroking her chin and huffing as if she were about to strike something with her blasted cane. The woman had cause to hate the Campbells. Not only did the late Earl of Argyll lay siege to Toward Castle with cannons, fire, and sword, he'd decimated an entire clan. Alice's clan. During the siege, Sir James Lamont had ordered his wife to take their only grandchild and spirit her out the secret passageway to the hidden cellars, the same route Alice had used that very day. Praying for a miracle, Gran had taken the newborn bairn and hid.

That fateful day all had been lost. When Gran's husband, the feared knight and Lamont chieftain, negotiated the terms of surrender, he'd given up his castle and livestock to preserve the lives of his clan. But no, not even evicting his enemy from his land had been enough to satisfy the earl. Argyll's bloodlust proved far too great to merely accept surrender of lands and livestock of an entire clan.

Alice gripped her stomach as her mind fixed upon the story. No matter how much she tried to steel her nerves, the brutal truth always made her blood pulse with ice.

After Grandfather had conceded defeat, Argyll marched the Lamonts to the churchyard in Dunoon. There the earl brutally executed every man, woman and child and then commanded his men to put all Lamont lands to fire and sword while Gran remained tucked away deep in the caverns below Toward Castle where she remained with Alice for an entire year. Only when it was safe did she take her granddaughter to the cottage in the wood.

Shaking off the chill, Alice poured herself another cup of water. "They're going to the fête at Rothesay Castle, I'm certain of it."

Gran leaned heavily on her cane, her gnarled fingers wrapped around the worn crook. "How do ye ken?"

"I heard them talking."

"Good heavens, child. You could have been smote where you stood."

"I hid in the cellars. Heard every word."

"You are careless."

"Nay!" Alice's ears rang, and this from the brave woman who'd saved her from the massacre. "How can you say such a thing? You hid in the cellars with *me*."

"That was long ago, afore the keep completely fell into ruin." Gran slid onto the bench beside Alice. "Tell me what they said."

"They were talking about me, mostly. One of them saw me in the clearing and then made chase."

Clapping a hand over her heart, Gran pretended to swoon. "My word, it grows worse."

"Nay, the others decided the heir had seen a selkie."

"Heir?"

"Aye, one man called the leader 'your lordship' and the other referred to himself as the second son—and then they decided to set up camp for the night. Then the Campbell heir started ordering the others about." Alice decided against telling Gran the man in charge had been ever so braw and strikingly handsome with his thick chestnut hair clubbed back. Such an admittance would reveal exactly how close she'd been to the scoundrels. And their looks mattered not. All three were knaves and scoundrels.

Gran leaned on her cane, her lips twisted as if deep in thought. "Two of Argyll's offspring will be sleeping in Toward Castle this very night?"

"Aye. What can we do?" Alice sprang to her feet and pounded her fist on the table. "This is our chance for vengeance—our chance to repay the crimes against Grandad, my father, and our clan."

"If he is the heir to the earldom, then it is Quinn Campbell who is sleeping in the remains of a once great and powerful clan, the grandson of Archibald the black-hearted beast."

"Quinn, aye?" Alice wasn't overly anxious to know the

man's name. He might be pleasing to the eye, but he was the spawn of the devil and she doubted he'd be alive come dawn. "Nightshade might do the trick."

"Nay." Gran pulled Alice out to the garden. Oddly, she didn't stop by the plot with medicinal herbs—the plot with a clump of nightshade and a wee clump of hemlock. Hobbling along, she kept going until she reached the stone fence. There she gestured to a spindly bush of thorns with but a half-dozen leaves.

"After two and twenty years, my demask rose has finally produced a bud," Gran said, her voice soft, as if she'd nurtured a plant from a seed to a glorious masterpiece.

"Rose?" Alice asked, bending over and carefully pulling aside the neighboring clump of gorse. "Ah, there it is."

"Aye, it's been hiding from me, the elusive bloom. I discovered it only yesterday." Gran cradled the bud as if it were as precious as a ruby. "I purchased this bush from a passing tinker and planted it on your second birthday."

"And it hasn't yielded a single flower until now? Looking as pallid as it does, I'm surprised the thing lived so long."

"Hmm. Sometimes it takes a lifetime to nurture a living soul until it yields its fruit."

"You speak as if the rosebush is human."

"It could be our salvation."

"Goodness, Gran. You make no sense at all."

"Perhaps not, but you will take this rosebud and leave it beside Quinn Campbell as he sleeps this night."

Alice gasped so violently, she nearly toppled. "I beg your pardon? I love you more than anyone in all of Christendom, but have ye gone daft?"

"Not in the slightest." The old woman's eyes flashed as she shook her cane. "You were just there today, were you not?"

As the makeshift weapon hissed through the air, Alice backed away from the crook before it jabbed her nose. "Aye and you chided me for it. I cannot creep up on His Lordship. What if he wakes?"

"You must be certain all are fast asleep afore ye near him. Wait until the wee hours, step softly and do not make a sound."

"Might I take a dirk? I'd rather run a blade across his throat than give him a thorny rose." As she spoke, Alice's stomach turned over. Somehow the idea of having the man's blood on her hands didn't sit well. It was one thing to lace the burn with a wee bit of poison on the off chance it might make the men a tad ill, but to smite him with her hands? She couldn't do it, even if the man was a Campbell.

"You will not touch him," Gran continued. "Whilst he slumbers, whisper that the rose is a gift from the selkies they were so anxious to find—from the *queen* of the selkies."

"But what if I wake him? Shall I tell him I'm a selkie... strike fear in his heart? Say if he touches me he'll not live to see the sunrise?"

"I hope he doesn't wake." Gran tapped her fingers together as if she were scheming. "In fact, I'll wager he will not."

"But what if he does?"

"The rose is your protection."

Rolling her eyes, Alice couldn't help but snort. "A thorny bud that looks as if it will wilt afore it blooms?"

"Calm yourself and cease your worry." Gran grasped her shoulders. "Before you leave him, you must repeat these words whether he wakes or not: *It is a wise man who can harness the power of the rose. Brawn and bravery may come and go but only wisdom can reverse the curse.*"

"Curse?" Alice examined the bud more closely. It wasn't red. Closed, it looked almost blue—violet, perhaps, like no rosebud she'd ever seen. "Are you casting a charm? One that will send a blight over the heir and his kin?"

"Not exactly." Gran snipped the stem, her lips pursed as if she'd already divulged more about the cryptic rose than she cared to. "I'm testing the waters is all."

"Are you not feeling well?" Alice asked, quite certain Gran might be growing a tad senile. "I think you might need a tonic."

Ignoring her remark, the dear woman examined the stem. "Good, there are plenty of thorns."

"If you ask me there's nothing but thorns to that rosebush. We'd be better off planting some avens in its place or at least something useful."

"Oh, no. Not after all these years. I will see justice. I swear it."

Her grandmother grew more cryptic by the moment. She was pleased with the thorns on some worthless, spindly rosebush? "Just testing the waters?" Afraid to touch the bloom, Alice eyed it, and whispered, "Is there poison in the thorns?"

"Of sorts, but it ought not kill him. Now do as I say and ask no more questions."

Chapter Two

Alice waited in the old cellars at least an hour after the men's quiet banter faded and surrendered to nighttime sounds of crickets and frogs. Of leaves whispering in the breeze, and the rhythmic cadence of the surf in the distance. To add to the concert, the chilly air resounded with light, masculine snores. She moved up the stairs only far enough to part the vines and peer across to the men, wrapped in their plaids. A crackling fire illuminated their forms, two on their sides sleeping with their backs to the flame. But one of the three lay only paces away, slumbering on his back as if the fire had made him overwarm. He was a large man, but not as rotund as the largest.

She instantly recognized the man on his back as Quinn Campbell. He had a full head of chestnut hair with blue moonlight dancing through the thick waves. An imposing Highlander, his plaid did nothing to hide the brawn beneath. Sword and musket at his side, doubtless he had a dirk hidden in close reach. Perhaps the blade was secure in his hand under the woolen folds?

To keep the rosebud alive, Gran had wrapped the stem in

linen soaked in a tincture of willow bark, secured it with a bit of oiled leather and tied the lot with a thong.

Not daring to stand to her full height, she crept to the man's side and kneeled. His eyes were closed, his lips half parted and in slumber he looked as gentle as a lamb. But she knew better. This man was a monster.

The rose trembled in her fingers. "I'm nay supposed to wake ye, but I'll have ye ken you're trespassing on Lamont lands. No matter who holds the deed, this very ground will always be stained with the blood spilled by your grandfather —the blood of my kin."

Emboldened by her words, Alice set the rose atop Quinn Campbell's chest and repeated the words Gran had insisted she say, "*It is a wise man who can harness the power of the rose. Brawn and bravery may come and go but only wisdom can reverse the curse.*"

"Who are you?" His Lordship asked, his voice but a whisper no louder than the breeze.

Alice's heart flew to her throat as she crouched and eased away, her gaze darting to his face. Blessed be the saints, he hadn't opened his eyes.

Growing emboldened, she moistened her lips. "I'm a selkie, come to tell ye to leave this place and never return."

"But these are my lands," he said as clear as day, though he made not a twitch.

Alice slunk toward the shadows. "Lands stolen by disgrace and tyranny will *never* be yours."

As the young lord's eyes blinked open, Alice slipped away as quietly as she'd come.

༄

QUINN JOLTED UPRIGHT.
What the blazes?

He shoved the hair away from his face, trying to recall the damned dream. At least he'd thought he'd had the most vivid dream of his life until he noticed a flower had dropped to his lap as he'd sat up. He grasped the stem and a vicious thorn stabbed his finger.

"Ow."

Quinn wiped the blood on his plaid, then gingerly pinched the part of the stem wrapped in leather and held it toward the moonlight. Unbelievable. He'd expected a bloom of unearthly magnificence, but he held nothing but a sickly-looking rosebud.

But the bonny lass had brought it. He knew it in his bones. She'd come to him. The same woman he'd seen in the forest had spoken to him in hushed, sultry tones.

In a blink, he realized she'd fled yet again.

No!

Casting aside his blanket, Quinn raced up to the crumbling wall-walk. Where was she? Why had she come? And just when he'd began to stir, she'd run. Why?

He needed to talk to the lass, ask her name. Look into her eyes. He must find out more about the beauty. Where was she from? Why was she alone? Did she need assistance, sustenance?

Damnation!

Why was he so drawn to her? He'd seen only long, silken tresses, a blue gown, and indescribable radiance. He'd stolen only a glimpse, but she was the bonniest creature to walk the Highlands. He was certain of it right down to his toes.

Something flickered in the distance. Blonde hair?

Was it she?

Quinn raced down the steps, stooping to pick up his sword and belt as he dashed past his pallet. He sprinted toward the flicker he'd seen. Branches slapped his face. The thorns of gorse scraped his legs while he leapt over logs and boulders.

Never slowing, he searched the shadows, his eyes wide, missing nothing.

Where are you?

His lungs burned, but Quinn refused to slow his pace until he reached a sandy beach, the Firth of Clyde stretching before him. Gasping for air, he stopped with his hands on his knees, the surf gently sliding over his leather boots with a rush of seafoam.

But the blood rushing in his veins was anything but gentle. It pounded through his heart and in his head, thrumming while he walked the length of the shore. "I do not believe in selkies!" he bellowed, his words swallowed by the breaking waves. "I do not believe in fairies, either!"

Quinn kicked the sand with a roar. He picked up a rock and threw it out to sea. "Arrggh!"

Another thorn pricked his finger. Again, he studied the bud in the moonlight. As if by magic, he saw the woman in his mind's eye. Yes, her hair had attracted him at first, but her face was ethereal like an angel. Her skin had a pearlescent luminescence oddly without blemish. Her lips were pink and her eyes dark like Highland blaeberries. And beneath her blue kirtle, her body was lean, but not too thin. Aye—a small waist supported by rounded hips.

With his next inhale, he vowed to find her.

He would see the woman again. He felt it in his bones. There was a reason she'd come to him. What had she said? Something about honor, kin, and blood spilled. Of her softspoken words, there was one passage that struck a chord—something about harnessing the power of the rose—not through force, but through wisdom. And something about a curse.

What curse?

Quinn rubbed the back of his neck and stared out to sea. Next time he'd not allow the fair maiden to slip through his grasp so easily.

But how? They were off to the Isle of Bute on the morrow. If he tarried, he'd miss the gathering and his chance to defend his title. Curse it, he might have to wait until he returned to the mainland, but make no bones about it, Quinn vowed to find her.

Chapter Three

After crossing the Clyde, a laborer on the pier caught the ferry's rope as the sailors furled the sails. The flat-bottomed boat rocked erratically with the lapping of the surf. Quinn gripped his horse's bridle while stroking his neck to keep the beast calm. "Easy laddie. We'll step ashore in no time."

MacGregor's old nag seemed unperturbed as she stood with her head lowered. Glenn hadn't even bothered to hold the mare's reins. "I can smell the roasting pork from here."

"All I can smell is seaweed and dead fish," said Eachan.

Though Quinn didn't care for naysayers, this time he had to agree with his brother. By the stench and number of fishing vessels they'd seen on the crossing, the herring trade was thriving on the Isle of Bute as it should be on the peninsula of Dunoon. With much of Scotland still suffering from the aftermath of Cromwell's war, it was good to see the bustling seaside village of Rothesay and the moated castle posing a picturesque backdrop.

"Have a look, lads." Quinn pointed. "The Campbell pennant is flying from the tower."

"Will you be competing in the games this year, m'lord?" asked the ship's master.

"Bloody oath. I've a title to defend."

Grinning, MacGregor ran his fingers through his horse's mane. "Ye mean, a title to lose."

Though Glenn was a commendable adversary, Quinn couldn't let his friend's comment slip by without a rebuttal. "Always nipping at my heels, are you not?"

"Someone needs to keep your ego from growing too large."

"Oh aye, so you've appointed yourself keeper of my conscience, have you?"

"After last year, someone needed to."

"You're full of shite."

"And you're full of..." MacGregor slapped his hand through the air. "Och, never ye mind. Whatever the source of that foul stench, you're full of it."

Quinn laughed. The three of them might poke fun, but the bond between the men was as solid as granite. He'd known MacGregor since they were both in swaddling. Glenn was as much a brother to him as Eachan—possibly more so.

A sailor slid the gangway across to the pier and Quinn thanked the crew, giving each a coin before he and his companions led their horses to dry land. Once ashore, they followed the more pleasant scent of rich food wafting from High Street until they found the merchant tents displaying their market-day wares.

"Saddles made to order here," beckoned a vendor. "I have everything a horseman needs, stirrup leathers, blankets, and bridles."

Quinn gave the man a nod and kept going, his friends at his flanks. Though he hadn't told them about his brush with the woman last eve, his gaze never stopped scanning the grounds for the lass. It wasn't likely she'd made the crossing for the fête, but not impossible. Nonetheless, once the games were over, he intended to pay a visit to Toward on his own and find the woman.

"I'm heading for the food tent," Eachan said, riding ahead. "Whatever they're cooking is making my mouth water."

MacGregor's horse stepped up the pace as well. "Agreed. I've been starved since we left Inveraray."

"You're always hungry." Intending to follow, Quinn slapped his reins. But when an elderly woman using a cane hobbled into his path, he quickly pulled his horse to a stop. "Whoa."

For an instant, she looked startled, but her eyes quickly shifted to the rosebud he'd pinned at his shoulder with his clan brooch. "The flower has begun to open," she said as if she had given him the bud herself.

Quinn immediately dismounted. "You know of this rose?"

"I do. 'Tis a damask rose. One that only blooms when it has mind to do so."

Reins in hand, he glanced in the direction of the food tent. "You make no sense at all. Flowers don't bloom whenever they *feel* the need."

"I think I'm being perfectly reasonable, m'lord. In fact, all flowers only bloom for a reason. Though the damask rose is the rarest and most elusive."

Quinn moved closer, his mind calculating. "And the woman who brought it last eve. Where might I find her?"

Thumping her cane on the ground, she snorted. "Ah, a young man chasing a bonny lass. Some things never change."

"Do you know her?"

"Perhaps. Come with me, m'lord." She hobbled toward an open tent, bearing a sign that read, "*Asketh thy Seer*".

The woman seemed far shrewder than by first glance. It hadn't escaped Quinn's notice when she'd called him lord. She knew who he was, which he hadn't expected. Certainly, he was the heir to the Argyll title, but he hadn't been to Rothesay since he was a lad. True, he had come to the games to uphold the title he'd earned last year, but those events had been in Dalmally on Loch Awe.

"Who are you?" he asked, following the woman into the tent. "Can you divine the future?"

"Hmm. This is a fête and what would a gathering be without an old woman foretelling things that may come?" She sat in a rickety old chair beside a table, then gestured to a half-barrel on the other side. "Sit. Do not make me crane my neck."

"You didn't answer my question." Quinn sat on the barrel, so low, his knees came up to his chin. "Do ye ken who gave me the bud?"

"I have an idea."

He shifted, sitting taller. "Do not be cryptic with me."

The woman rapped his knee with her blasted cane. "And do not be domineering with me, young whelp or that rose tucked in your brooch will never bloom."

Quinn rubbed his knee. "Why should I give a rat's arse if it blooms or nay?"

"I beg your pardon, m'lord, but I am no wench who enjoys coarse language."

"Forgive me." He gestured to the flower. "Please enlighten me as to why I should concern myself with the welfare of this thorny rose."

"Have the thorns pierced your skin?"

"More than once."

"Good."

"I think not—they gave me welts." Quinn rubbed his sore fingers together. "Why is this bloom so important?"

"Your father is arrogant and self-serving. In my experience the acorn never falls far from the tree."

"My father?" He shook his head and stared at the shrew.

"Madam, your banter is making me dizzy. If you think so ill of the earl, then why are we having this discussion?"

"Because you are not beyond saving. Yet."

"I've had enough." Quinn pushed to his feet. "You speak in riddles and by the sign on the tent, I reckon ye are a witch. I'd watch myself if I were you."

"Spoken like a true Campbell."

"Bloody oath, woman. You have the most maddening way of raising my ire."

As he started away, she caught his wrist with the hook of her cane. "He who dares grasp the thorn will become the instrument of peace, but he who shuns it will only serve to increase the hatred between clans."

He looked her from head to toe. What was she about? Was she deliberately trying to unnerve him? And why was she mumbling all this rubbish about peace and hatred? Unless she was... "You're a Lamont," he growled.

With a gap-toothed grin, she leaned in. "Och aye, and do ye ken what happened in May four and twenty years past?"

Jesu, everyone knew of the Dunoon Massacre. It had posed a black mark on the Campbell name for two generations. Quinn's grandfather massacred nearly the entire Lamont clan, including the chieftain. Only a few had escaped and those who did were thought to have fled to the Lowlands.

The way the woman stared at him with ice in her eyes did not seem of this world. He narrowed his gaze as he backed out the tent's flap. "Are you a spirit come to haunt me?"

"I am an old woman who has lived a life of misery and sorrow." She flicked her cane toward Quinn's horse. "I have shown you to the path of your salvation. Whether or not you choose to take it is up to you. Are you a merciful man, or are you a tyrant?"

"I am a Campbell," he growled, reaching for his mount's reins.

"Perhaps you are, but I'll not hold such malfeasance against you—not this day. You, sir, hold the power to change your destiny." She grasped his wrist and squeezed. "If you're nay too bull-headed to see the opportunity when 'tis laid out before you."

He shook his arm free and mounted. But as he rode away, the woman's words needled like a swarm of bees attacking every inch of Quinn's flesh.

❧

NEARLY TIME FOR THE OPENING CEREMONY, ALICE hastened through the maze of tents, clutching tight her basket of herbs. Never in her life had she seen so many people gathered in one place. It was like an ant hill with humanity everywhere. Though this was an annual gathering, it was the first time she and Gran had attended—primarily because it was sponsored by the Earl of Argyll. Oddly, Alice's grandmother had insisted they come because this year it was but a short ferry ride across the Clyde. All Highland clans were welcome, or so said the posting on the church door.

Truth be told, Gran had decided it was time for Alice to be introduced to society, as it were. A handful of families lived in Toward, but no lads her age. Gran had insisted that at four and twenty, Alice was on the verge of spinsterhood which was not acceptable for the Lamont heir and it was high time for Alice to marry.

Marriage.

Good heavens, the thought of finding a spouse made perspiration spring across her skin. Who would want to marry Alice anyway? She might be the sole heir to the chieftainship, but she had naught but a plaid and brooch to show for it.

As she rounded the corner and started into the tent, she stopped dead in her tracks, the basket in her arms nearly tumbling to the ground. Merciful fairies, Lord Quinn was sitting beside Gran having a wee chat.

Backing as fast as she could, Alice bumped into a Highlander, some the contents of her basket spilling.

"Watch yourself," growled the man.

She hardly acknowledged him as she skirted around to the side of the tent, her ears pricked, listening to Gran's banter, not certain if their conversation was friendly or not.

"...Are you a merciful man or are you a tyrant?" Gran's parting words sounded more like a challenge before His Lordship briskly marched out of the tent.

Still crouching, Alice raised the basket to hide her face. Yes, she knew Lord Quinn would be at the fête, but the last place she expected to see him was in her tent talking to Gran. It was a wonder the old woman hadn't tried to give him a tincture laced with nightshade as Alice had suggested. Clearly, her grandmother had something up her sleeve—and it didn't appear to encompass the end of Lord Quinn's life. Further, Gran had spoken to the heir to the earldom of Argyll speaking with the same cryptic nonsense she'd used with Alice. Och aye, the woman was scheming for certain. The quandary? What in heaven's name was she about? And why was the thorny rose at the center of it?

Aye, they'd put up a sign on the tent to tell fortunes and earn a bit of coin. But Gran was no witch. True, she was a bit odd at times, and she knew more about herbs and remedies than most anyone but that was the extent of it.

Alice lowered her basket and, after checking to ensure Lord Quinn was long gone, she slipped into the tent and set the herbs she'd purchased beside the bedrolls. "I saw Quinn Campbell leave a moment ago."

Gran arched an eyebrow. "Did you now?"

"Aye." Alice stood with her hands on her hips giving her grandmother a hard stare. "Now tell me true, what is it you are planning for his demise? Is there something in that rose that will slowly take away his breath? Will he fail at the games? Will his death be agonizingly painful?"

Pursing her lips, Gran's face wrinkled like a prune. "He's not going to die. At least not by my hand."

"I beg your pardon? Of all the people at this *ceilidh*, you have more cause to hate him than anyone."

"Is that what you think? That hate is the answer? That the Lamonts should feud with the Campbells for the rest of eternity?"

"Of course—" Alice clenched her teeth and set to fishing in her valise for a hairbrush.

Bless it, at times Gran was infuriating. Could there ever be a truce between the Campbells and the Lamonts? After they mercilessly massacred her clan? She'd lived her life in a shabby cottage. Aye it was cozy, but thanks to the Campbells, Alice had been deprived of growing up in fine style. She'd been deprived of lavish gowns and a marriage arranged to strengthen bonds between clans. Her mother had died in childbirth, but her very own father had lost his life in battle with the Campbells—Lord Quinn's kin.

Could Alice ever put the past behind her? She'd been an infant when Archibald Campbell had mercilessly struck in the dead of night with no warning.

Could she ever forgive? Or was the tonic too bitter?

Four and twenty years had passed since that fateful day, but it may as well have been a fortnight.

Chapter Four

"Merciful fairies," Alice whispered behind clenched fists. She knew Lord Quinn to be a powerful man, but she never would have guessed he possessed the strength to nearly double any other man's mark in the stone put. God might strike her dead for admiring the man—either God or Gran, but how could anyone help but do so? Besides, it was good to develop healthy respect for the strengths of one's adversary. Right. That's all she was doing and absolutely nothing more.

Making Alice all the more self-aware, dear Gran sat beside her and watched every bit as intently.

They'd chosen a place atop the hill away from the crowds. Behind them loomed the partially ruined Rothesay Castle. The medieval fortress was no longer occupied, though her walls were in far better condition than Toward Castle. And tonight the men would build a bonfire in the courtyard. Alice was looking forward to the music and dancing, and especially the pork which the lads had been turning on the spit all day.

"That Highlander is quite braw," Gran mumbled.

Alice gaped, feigning ignorance. "To whom are you referring?"

The old woman met her stare with a wizened one. "You cannot fool me, lass."

"I beg your pardon?"

"He's the most handsome man at the fête." She pointed to a gathering of girls all giggling and waving their kerchiefs at Lord Quinn as he held up his arms in victory. "Look at those lassies making fools of themselves."

Simply watching their shamelessness lassies made her skin hot. "They can have him."

"Mm hmm."

Feigning indifference, Alice adjusted her arisaid about her shoulders. And she didn't care much for the smug expression on Gran's face, either. "He came in second in the footrace."

"And first in archery."

"Pardon me, but if I didn't know you better, I'd think you were trying to make me like him."

"Oh aye?" Gran bit into an oatcake. "I thought we were having a conversation about how well the Campbell heir was faring. As a matter of fact, I reckon he'll be the victor again this year."

It was likely he'd win the caber toss, and that would seal it...unless something drastic happened like his mount coming up lame in the horse race. With all the jumps planned, such a thing could happen.

"I don't suppose it matters overmuch to us who wins, as long as the Campbells go back to Inveraray and leave us be." Alice snatched the last oatcake and shook it. "And I'm not about to deliver any more roses in the middle of the night. That rose didn't do a thing to him, except mayhap make him stronger."

"I assure you, he is unchanged."

"Then why did you send me?"

"Because I thought there might be hope."

Nibbling her oatcake, Alice studied her grandmother. "Hope for what?"

"Never you mind." Uprighting her cane, Gran started to rise. "Come, lass, 'tis time to dress for the *ceilidh*."

"Dress?" Alice hopped to her feet and helped her grandmother stand. "'Tis a gathering, nay a fancy ball."

"Thank the good Lord for small mercies."

᠃

Tankard in hand, Eachan led the way through the maze of people. "I reckon you ought to find something else with which to occupy your time next year and give the rest of us bleating sops a chance."

"A bit jealous, are you?" asked Quinn as he passed his brother and headed for the long row of tables reserved for attending chieftains and gentry.

A lass rose from a plaid she was sharing with her family and curtsied. "Good evening, m'lord."

Though he didn't stop, Quinn bowed his head respectfully. "Good evening."

Of course, Eachan stopped and grasped the girl's hand. "And a fine night it is, especially with you making it so."

Good God, his younger brother ought to be a bard. The lad flaunted his charm to every lassie who crossed his path.

Let Eachan have his fun. Quinn hadn't an eye for just *any* lassie this eve. After his wee chat with the old seer, he hadn't stopped searching for a bonny blonde wearing a blue dress. To his chagrin, when he'd been named grand champion too many women had surrounded him, each one paling in comparison to the nymph who'd given him the rose. He glanced at the flower still pinned at his shoulder. It had opened a bit more and, bless it, the bloom had taken on a healthier glow.

"Och, if it is not the behemoth himself," said Rory MacLeod, chieftain of Clan MacLeod of Harris.

Sliding onto the seat beside the man, Quinn gestured for MacGregor to join them. Eachan would follow in his own time—when he finished slavering over the lassies no doubt.

A serving wench placed tankards of ale in front of them. "What's this?" Quinn asked. "The way everyone is carrying on, you'd think I'm akin to Goliath."

"Ye are," grumbled MacDougall across the board.

Quinn took a healthy drink of ale. "Not by half. And MacGregor's a hand taller," he said, stealing a glance over each shoulder.

Where is she?

The courtyard suddenly grew quiet and all eyes shifted to the arched entry. Sitting a bit taller, Quinn looked as well.

And then he saw her. The woman from the forest. The nymph who visited Quinn's dreams. His heart thudded against his chest. His mouth grew dry.

"God's bones," he blurted, his skin growing hot.

"Aye," said MacGregor in a tone so lecherous, it immediately made Quinn want to throw a jab across the lout's jaw.

The goddess moved gracefully the entire length of the hall until she reached the high table. She stood at the far end like she belonged—mayhap as if she were above them all. A bumbling servant pulled out a chair and bowed. But she didn't sit immediately. Her gaze swept across the laird's faces, stopping when those captivating sapphire eyes met Quinn's. In a heartbeat his breath caught as if she'd slayed him. Would he be begging for the scraps from her plate by the night's end?

Aye, I'd beg on my knees if she'd allow me five minutes to gaze into her eyes.

She embodied the regality of a Scottish queen, wearing a crown of red roses, a gown with a snug fitting bodice, and a blue and green plaid fastened at her shoulder with a chieftain's brooch with four emeralds—one as bold as Quinn's.

"A woman clan chief?" mumbled MacGregor. "Bloody figures."

But Quinn paid him no mind. What he wanted to know was why had the lass appeared alone in the forest? Especially if she was highborn. Why had she brought the rosebud to him last eve? Blessed be the saints, the woman defined beauty. Beneath her circlet, the nymph wore her hair unbound. Aye, the cascades of waves flowing all the way to her hips made every man in the hall weak at the knees. A medieval princess presiding over a medieval castle could not be more fitting for this eve.

What were the words she'd said?

Quinn's mind couldn't focus, but he knew his victory that day had not impressed her. Aye, dozens of women around would give their eyeteeth to lie with him this night, but not a one would suffice but the beauty who gazed upon him without a smile. Did she harbor some dark secret about him that was too horrible to utter?

"Who is she?" he asked MacLeod.

"I have no idea," Quinn mumbled, unable to avert his gaze.

Down the table, the rest of the men appeared to be baffled as well, but nary a one spoke out.

Quinn spent the rest of the meal watching her. She rarely glanced his way, but when she did, his heart pounded like the thundering of a racehorse.

"You aiming to eat that?" asked MacGregor.

He blinked. "Huh?"

The henchman pointed with his fork. "The pound of pork

on your plate. Bloody oath, after the day's activity, I would have thought you'd be famished."

Quinn pushed the food toward his friend. "Take it."

When finally the pipers and fiddlers announced a reel, he sprang to his feet and boldly strode toward the lass. A delicate eyebrow arched as he executed a courtly bow. "May I have the honor of this dance?"

When she hesitated, the chieftain beside her leaned in. "It would be disrespectful to refuse His Lordship."

"Nay," Quinn said. "I want only what the lady desires."

"What I desire, m'lord?" she asked in the same sultry tone he'd thought he dreamed the night before.

"Aye, for I believe a woman of your ilk should not be cosseted by the rules that bind mere mortals."

Enticing blue eyes grew darker. "I assure you, I am as mortal as you, perhaps more so."

"Perhaps, but this night you are not of this world." He bowed, deeper this time. "Please dance with me, m'lady."

BY THE TIME ALICE PLACED HER FINGERS IN LORD QUINN'S outstretched palm, she was shaking like a sapling in a gale-force wind.

Curses to Gran for putting her up to this. Since she'd stepped into the hall everyone had been was staring at her as if she were the queen of the fairies. Moreover, they acted as if she would smite them if anyone uttered a criticizing word. Had Toward Castle not been burned, had the Lamont lands not been stolen, Alice might be a force to be reckoned with, but without them she was nothing. She was nothing but a poor maid who had grown up hiding from her enemies—people like Quinn Campbell who presently held her hand, leading her to the round patch of grass where the dancers were congregating for a reel.

With bold strides, His Lordship escorted her to the lady's line. Before he left to join the men, he leaned forward and whispered, "Pray tell, what is your name?"

"Alice," she replied, his closeness making her tremble all the more.

"Merely Alice?"

"Aye."

The music demanded he accept her response and join the men's line. Taller and bonnier than the others, he stood there like a king, his gaze not leaving her face even after they began to dance. Intense and focused, his eyes were a rich mahogany, nearly the same color as his hair. He danced like a competitor, his motion crisp and accurate while his kilt slapped the back of his legs. During the turns, he grasped her hand firmly though gently enough not to cause pain.

Alice didn't want to like him, but it was impossible not to fall victim to the handsome contours of his face. Rather than a periwig, he wore his hair clubbed back, though a wave falling to the side of his chiseled cheek had escaped. It gave him an air of wildness, which combined with the shadow of his beard, made him almost irresistible. Had the man not been a Campbell, Alice doubted she'd be able to move her feet.

"Are you enjoying the fête?" he asked, his deep brogue rolling off his tongue.

It didn't escape her notice that he'd mentioned nothing about the games earlier. "I have." Again, Alice chose brevity in her response. "And you?"

He grinned, a smile as brilliant as the sun set her stomach aflutter. "I suppose I haven't had much time to consider it."

"Does the competition make you nervous?"

"Not overmuch. I hate to lose, though, so I suppose—"

His words were cut off by the need to skip along with the woman to Alice's right while she locked elbows with a man she'd never seen before.

Out of the corner of her eye, she assessed the new man, hoping to find him attractive, yet she was unduly disappointed. She couldn't hide her smile when she again joined hands with His Lordship.

His eyes twinkled. "You're the bonniest woman here," he whispered, his breath skimming her neck.

Merciful fairies, why not allow herself to like this man, just for tonight? The thought made her search the faces for Gran. She must be lurking somewhere in the shadows. Alice had been dismayed when her grandmother had pushed her toward the *ceilidh* alone. If only they could have gone in together. But the wizened woman had been emphatic that Alice must join the clan chiefs alone without letting anyone know who she truly was.

Aye, by the end of the evening, she might mention she was the sole Lamont heir, but not until.

Pinned at Quinn's shoulder, the damask looked incredibly vibrant. How could the rose grow so much more radiant after it had been plucked? Would it bloom in full this night, or would there be more? Of one thing Alice was sure: if Quinn Campbell continued to command her time, she had absolutely no chance of finding a suitor.

Chapter Five

Command her time, His Lordship certainly did. And there wasn't anything Alice could do about it. Had she forgotten how to say no? By the time the music stopped, she'd almost lost sight of the powerful hatred between their clans or that Lord Quinn still had no idea she was a Lamont.

Nearly out of breath, she curtsied. "Thank you for—"

Crack!

Within a blink, Alice crouched, drawing her fists beneath her chin. The musket blasted from the wall-walk. A lead ball whistled over Alice's head. Before her eyes, the shot thudded into her dancing partner's shoulder. Hurtled backward, His Lordship's smile distorted into a grimace of shock and pain. Arms flailing, he crashed to the ground as more shots boomed from above.

A woman screamed.

Alice's throat burned as if she'd been the one screaming.

Time slowed as the courtyard plunged into utter mayhem. Alice stared in disbelief. Oh, God. Quinn Campbell had been shot. All around the courtyard, long tables crashed to their sides as Highlanders charged their muskets and returned fire.

With her next blink, Alice dove on top of Quinn to protect him from the volley of fire. "Help!" she shouted.

The big man shifted beneath her. "I'm all right, lass," he grunted. But he wasn't.

She spotted stone wall only five paces away—safety. "Can you rise?"

"As long as I'm breathing I'll fight to the end."

Musket fire blasted from all directions.

"You've no weapons save your dirk!" she shrieked.

"That can be remedied." Even facing death with blood seeping through his doublet, the man was cocksure.

Alice shifted aside. He'd lost too much blood. He might be talking like a warrior now, but as soon as he tried to stand he'd find himself far weaker than he believed. She took his hand and squeezed. "On the count of three, follow me."

"But I—"

"Three!" With no time to argue, she sprang to her feet and tugged his hand.

Wincing, he stood.

In a crouch, she tugged him toward the safety of the wall —an alcove of some sort. "This way."

"Over here!" Gran called from a cavern no more than three feet high, as if she'd been hiding in that spot. Had she expected this?

Surely not.

"Come!" Alice shouted, glancing over her shoulder and veering toward the wee cavern. His Lordship followed, his face blanched but determined.

"Haste," Gran ushered them inside. "This way."

The clashing sounds of battle grew muffled as they fled through the gap in the wall. Alice kept a tight hold on Quinn's hand as Gran led them through a dank tunnel until it opened to the foregrounds.

"What's happening?" Alice looked twice at her grandmother, her head spinning. In place of her cane, the woman was holding a musket. "Are you a part of this?"

"Nay, but I'm not surprised." She tugged the pair toward the edge of the moat. "The water is only a few inches deep here. Go quickly. You'll find a skiff at the end of the pier. Spirit His Lordship across the Clyde. Stop for no one."

Resting his hands on his knees, Quinn shook his head. "I'm not leaving."

"Och aye, ye beast?" Gran challenged. "You aim to go back inside? They have the place surrounded and the only quarry they're after is you!"

Refusing to release Lord Quinn's hand, Alice surged ahead. "Who are those people?"

Gran lumbered beside her, leaning heavily on her musket. "They're rogues. I told them there was another way, but they refused to listen."

&

"Just because I am a woman doesn't mean I am helpless." Alice indignantly plopped her bottom on the rowing bench, jostling Quinn's injured shoulder. "And by the sound of the shouts coming from the castle, there is no time to argue."

His eyes watered as he bit back a bellow. "Och, have it your way." He picked up the oar and nearly roared again as white-hot pain shot through his entire body. He wasn't about to admit it, but the lass was right. His left arm had been rendered useless and tortured him as if impaled by an iron spike.

What else could go wrong? There he sat beside the woman who had filled his every thought for the past two days and now he'd been shot in the shoulder, pulling on an oar as they rowed a meager skiff toward the rough seas of the Clyde.

As they sailed out into Rothesay Bay, Quinn looked to the castle. Shouts of battle rose above the rush of the sea. Christ, he should be there fighting with Eachan and Glenn. And who the blazes had attacked a friendly gathering? Those miscreants had broken the code of Highland hospitality.

A hundred warring thoughts crowded his mind as men carrying torches raced for the shore.

"Row faster!" Alice shouted.

Quinn dragged his oar through the water with such force it made the boat veer toward the port side—Alice's side. "You should have let me row," he barked.

She gave her oar an impressive heave. "I can hold my own as well as anyone."

Shots blasted from the shore.

Quinn shoved the lass downward, covering her with his torso. "Take cover!"

For a moment the boat rocked in the water like a buoy. More shots rang out, but the boat remained sound. Quinn straightened and peered through the darkness. "I think we're out of range."

"Thank heavens."

Together they resumed rowing while torches flickered on the Rothesay shore, growing more distant by the moment.

"How are you faring?" Alice asked, her voice breathless. Aye, the lass was using every bit of strength she could muster, bless her.

"Fit enough to turn around and face those backbiters." Quinn ground his molars. If it weren't for the musket ball in his shoulder, he'd do just that. Truth be told, his strength was waning, his head out of sorts. He hated weakness. How much blood had he lost? Pints, no doubt and, by the sticky warmth of the shirt clinging to his shoulder, he reckoned the wound was still bleeding.

As they made the crossing, he shook his head several

times to stave off an overwhelming feeling of exhaustion. His entire body ached. His eyelids drooped as if ten-pound weights hung from each one.

God's bones, he should be in command of both oars. But no, instead he was rowing a skiff in tandem with the bonniest woman he'd ever seen in his life and he could barely hold his head up.

Bloody hero I am.

By the time the skiff skidded into the sand on the far shore, Quinn's chin was touching his chest. Grunting, he arched his eyebrows. "Give me a moment."

It took every bit of strength he could muster to step out of the boat into thigh-deep water. Something slippery made him loose his footing. With nothing to break his fall, Quinn bellowed a curse while he fell to his back. Icy saltwater flooded into his mouth and attacked his shoulder like daggers. The world spun as he tried to move his feet beneath him.

A hand grasped his wrist and tugged.

Keep fighting.

Quinn bore down, taking his weight onto his legs, while the woman slipped under his arm. "Stay with me a bit longer, m'lord. I'll have you to the cottage in no time."

Chapter Six

Alice staggered beneath the weight of the Highlander as she trudged toward the cottage. Even after he'd been shot and lost so much blood, Quinn had insisted on rowing. Didn't he think she could handle a wee boat? Alice was better at manning a skiff than riding a horse. And now when she needed the man to bear his weight, his strength was sapped. Worse, they were both dripping wet and freezing.

"Just a bit farther," she urged.

He grunted a reply, his eyes closed, his teeth chattering.

"There's the cottage just yonder." Alice strengthened her grip around Quinn's waist. "You're doing fine."

Though his feet continued to move, he uttered not a word. Only by the grace of God did they push through the cottage door.

Alice urged him onto the bench. "I'll make up a pallet in front of the hearth to warm you."

As soon as his weight eased from her shoulders, using flint and steel, she set to lighting the tallow candles with on the mantle. Quickly, she stacked flax tow and dry tender in the hearth. Lighting a twig in one of the candle's flames, she crouched down and ignited the bundle. In two blinks of an eye, the twigs were popping.

"It'll be warm in no time," she said as she angled two sticks of wood against each other so as not to snuff the wee flame.

Brushing off her hands, she chanced a look at His Lordship as she hastened past him. Heavens, the man was whiter than an apron hanging on the line in the afternoon sun. As fast as she could, she gathered an armful of pillows, linens and blankets from the cupboard.

Except when she returned, the Highlander was nowhere to be found. Alice turned full circle. "Your Lordship?"

Her toe hit something solid, followed by a resounding moan.

"Heaven's stars, could you not have waited five minutes afore you collapsed?"

"Sorry," he mumbled from the floor, though she couldn't be sure if he was conscious.

Alice swiftly made a pallet, then stood and regarded the very large, very wet man lying beside the table. Only about four feet from the makeshift bed, she tapped her fingers to her lips. "I reckon we need to remove your clothing, else you'll catch your death."

He didn't move—not even a twitch. "Mm," he moaned. At least he was still conscious.

She stooped and tugged his uninjured arm upward until she pulled him up enough to prop his back against the table leg.

"I'm going to remove your brooch and plaid," she explained, examining Quinn's plaid. As far as she could tell it was belted around his waist with the remaining length pulled across his back their backs and pinned at his shoulder.

She bit down on her lower lip as she unfastened the brooch. And when the damask rose fell into her palm, she snarled. "A lot of luck you've brought us." Shaking her head, she placed both the rose and brooch on the table, completely unable to fathom what her grandmother had been up to. Attending the fête proved a calamitous mistake. Alice should have stayed home and tended to her mending. Then she wouldn't be in this situation. And His Lordship mightn't have been shot.

"Can you unfasten your belt?" she asked, clasping her hands. "I'll avert my gaze and then you can slip under the blankets."

Of course, the daft Highlander chose now not to respond at all.

Her gaze slipped to the enormous silver buckle. Not only did it secure the man's kilt in place, this was Lord Quinn's belt. Of all the Highlanders in Scotland, the heir to the Campbell dynasty was bleeding and shivering in her wee cottage. Groaning, she looked to the rafters. "Merciful fairies, I'll do it."

Besides, because he is a Campbell, I shall be utterly unaffected by anything I might happen to see.

Aye, Alice thought herself an impenetrable fortress, especially when it came to this man...until, with one tug, the cloth dropped away, revealing a pair of muscular thighs peppered with dark hair. She'd never imagined a man's legs could be so powerful, so alluring. And aside from his shoes and hose, his only remaining garment was a long linen shirt covering the tops of his thighs. The wet cloth clung to his skin tightly and revealed every contour of his body beneath. The hole at the left shoulder was stained with blood, but just below the thick and fleshy muscles in his chest stood proud. At the tips were dark circles, nipples not much different than hers, but remarkably different at the same time. Her mouth grew dry as, unable to stop herself, her gaze drifted lower. His abdomen rippled with bands of sinew as if hewn from iron.

And lower... Holy everlasting father, lower. A dark triangle of hair shadowed his sex and there was absolutely no question about his manhood. This was as virile a man as ever walked the Highlands of Scotland.

Forcing her mouth to close, Alice wiped her eyes. "Ah...I suppose you may as well take off your shirt as well."

When he didn't respond, she removed his shoes and hose first, her gaze frequently flickering to his face to see if he might stir. She stood back and tapped her foot. *Come, ye beast. Do not make me strip ye completely bare.*

"Take off your shirt, Quinn!" she shouted.

The man's eyes flashed open. Shuddering, he whisked the garment over his head. "Arrgh!" he howled as the linen stuck to his wounded shoulder.

Alice held up her hand to shade her eyes from his...him... that... *Good Lord, are all men thus endowed?* "I'll finish."

She stripped away the shirt, leaving him completely nude. Trying not to ogle the poor injured soul, she urged him toward the pallet where she'd turned the blankets down. "I've made up a wee bed. I need you to shift yourself over there. Just a roll or two and you'll be toasty warm."

Somehow, he managed to inch over, though as soon as his bum hit the comfort of the pallet, he dropped to his back, sprawled like a spider.

Alice peeked at him through her fingers. "Ah...are you intending to stay in that position?"

Evidently, he was because His Lordship didn't bother to twitch.

"Very well." She picked up the blanket and dropped it over his lap.

After a healthy pat to her chest her heart returned to a somewhat normal cadence. She bent over his injured shoulder. It was angry red with traces of black powder encircling the puncture wound. Gingerly, she pressed her fingers around the flesh. Thankfully, the musket ball hadn't hit bone, but even Alice knew Quinn would die if the piece of lead weren't removed.

She looked to the door. If only Gran would have rowed across the firth with them. But surely she'd be along soon.

Alice puzzled for a moment. Why hadn't her grandmother accompanied them across the Clyde? There had been enough room in the skiff.

Why had she stayed behind?

❧

After the sun rose on the next morn, Gran still hadn't returned. Worse, Lord Quinn was sweating like a laborer in the hot sun.

"Water," he croaked, his voice nowhere as bold as it had been the previous day.

Cup in hand, Alice hastened to his side. "How are you feeling?"

He held his head up while she gave him a drink. "Like I've been shot."

"The ball needs to come out. It'll make you very ill if it does not."

He rested his head on the pillow and let out a long breath. "Have you experience with such a surgery?"

"I saw it done once." Gran had removed a musket ball from a man's knee, but he'd caught the fever all the same and died a month later. Alice bit her lip. No use telling Quinn his chances for survival were grim.

The blanket slipped lower as he traced his fingers around the wound. "Then you'll have to dig it out."

"Me?"

"Aye."

"My grandmother would do better. She's very skilled with the healing arts."

Quinn's gaze swept across the cottage. "I haven't seen her."

Alice offered him another sip. "I thought she would have come home by now."

"Are you worried?"

"Aye. She's been acting strangely as of late. I'm afraid she's going senile."

He licked the water from his cracked lips, his eyes losing focus for a moment. "In that case, I'd rather have you perform the deed. Then once I'm on my feet, we'll set out to find her."

"We?"

"Mm." He rubbed his arm right below the wound. "I'd reckon you'd want to go, would you not?"

"A-aye," Alice replied, none too convinced. She'd brought a Campbell into her home and now he was talking about taking her to search for Gran? Things were growing stranger by the moment.

"I'll fetch you something to help with the pain," she said, heading for the shed where Gran kept her medicine bundle and hung the herbs to dry. Unfortunately, the dear woman had never seen fit to record any of her remedies with quill and parchment.

Alice found the mortar and pestle and put it on the table while examining the stoppered pots. *Let's see...valerian, willow bark, a pinch of opium...* She chewed her lip as she looked at the vial of nightshade. Only a few days past she had thought to poison the man with it and now she was trying to save his life.

With a trembling hand, she pulled off the stopper and sprinkled in a tiny bit of the finely ground powder—any more and her remedy might be his undoing. Using the mortar, she mixed the tincture and then added a dram of whisky. Then she poured the lot into a cup and stirred it with her dagger for good measure. Alice had no idea why, but Gran always used her dagger to mix the tincture before she performed surgery, and now was no time to veer away from any matter of course.

Back inside the cottage, His Lordship gave the concoction a dubious look. "What's in it?"

"Whisky...mayhap a few pinches of this and that."

Scrunching his nose, he took the cup and held it aloft. "I can manage anything with a tot of spirit."

Alice said a silent prayer as she watched him drink.

"Ah." He wiped his mouth. "I wouldn't mind a bit more whisky if you have it."

"Perhaps after." She held up the dagger.

He cringed. "Blast. I'd hoped you might have forgotten about the wee lead ball."

"The sooner we have it out, the faster you'll heal." Kneeling beside him, she examined the wound. "Do you need a stick?"

"Nay."

But he hissed when she pressed her fingers around his wound. "Perhaps we should wait for the tincture to take effect," she suggested.

"Do it now afore I lose my nerve."

"You do not seem like a man who would lose his nerve easily, m'lord."

He grimaced as she located the ball just beneath the puncture. "I'm not," he grunted.

Steeling her nerves to keep her hands from trembling, she threw back her shoulders. "Gird yourself."

His lips formed a white line as his entire body tensed.

Alice clenched her teeth, levering the knife into the wound as she pressed hard against the lump.

Quinn made a gurgling sound of agony as his body jolted.

Alice flicked her wrist, but the ball slipped around the blade. "Curses." The word sounded strained as she worked the shot left then right while her patient writhed, baring his teeth.

"I nearly have it!" Pushing down, with one more dig of the blade, the slippery ball popped out.

"Satan's ballocks, that bloody hurt!" Quinn bellowed, his face blanching.

Pinching the round shot between her fingers, Alice couldn't help but grin. "At least it looks as if my tincture will nay kill you."

His fingers swathed a path through the blood pooling at his shoulder, spreading it across his chest. "Mayhap it will not. I reckon I'm more likely to bleed to death."

"Och, I'll nay allow it!" Springing to her feet, Alice grabbed a clean cloth from the pile of linens and pressed it firmly over the wound.

"Argh!": Gnashing his teeth, he arched upward, glaring like a madman. "Can you be a wee bit gentler, mind you?"

Alice pushed harder. "Forgive me, but we must staunch the bleeding."

With a defeated grunt, the big Highlander dropped his head to the pillow. "Where is it written goddesses have kind hearts?"

"I beg your pardon?"

"Athena was no shrinking violet."

Alice tossed the bloodied cloth aside and applied a fresh one. "You're making no sense at all."

Quinn's eyes rolled closed. "Mayhap on account..."

With his long exhale, her heart lurched with the force of a thunderbolt. "M'lord?"

Chapter Seven

❧

Quinn couldn't decide which was worse, the pounding in his head or the stabbing pain in his shoulder. Both tortured him relentlessly. Though when something soft pressed against his hip, he had a mind to open his eyes. Bugger the pain, something more feral filled his mind.

He inhaled deeply and the scent of wild berries soothed him. He opened one eye and smiled, stretching his parched lips. Fully clothed, Alice lay on her side with her back to him, her silken hair draped in wisps across her body. Her head rested on the crook of her arm. Above, a feminine shoulder gave way to a steep slope ending in a narrow waist and flaring into the most glorious hip.

"Are you real?" he whispered.

With a soft moan, she shifted, a lock of her hair falling onto Quinn's palm. He rubbed it between his fingers—so exquisitely soft. He drew the silken tress to his nose and inhaled heaven. "I think ye *are* a selkie, because you're too bonny to be of this world."

"Mm," her voice was rich and womanly, making him want to kiss her. But with another soft moan, she sat up and stretched. When she glanced his way, those beguiling blue eyes brightened just like a warm beam of sunshine. "Praises be, you're awake!"

"Was there any question?" he asked, his throat raspy and dry.

"Ah..." Her gaze trailed aside. "Let us just say I've been too worried to leave your side."

Quinn moved his toes. "How long have I been abed?"

"Two days."

"Two days? My kin will be sick with worry."

"*I* was sick with worry—and Gran still hasn't returned from Rothesay."

Draping his arm over his head, it all came back. Who the devil had shot him and why? *And the old woman had insisted the scoundrels were after me.*

"How is your shoulder?"

The damned thing seared with pain. "Hardly ken I've been shot."

"Truly? I've never seen a man recover so quickly."

He gave her a sheepish cringe. "Mayhap it'll be awhile afore I'm wrestling a colt."

"I would think so." She gestured to the table. "Are you hungry? Yesterday I made some bread and put a pot of mutton stew on to simmer."

Quinn's stomach growled at the mention of food. "I'm famished."

"Can you rise? I could bring a bowl and feed you here."

"I'll not be mollycoddled," he growled, trying to sound tougher than he felt. Honestly, having the lass spoon feed him while he reclined on the soft pillows was a far more enticing idea, but he'd never admit to it.

The pallet grew suddenly cold when Alice rose. "I'll dish up a couple of bowls."

"My thanks." He winced as he sat up, the blankets falling

to his hips. Och, he wore not a stich of clothing. Blast, his shirt and kilt were draped across a rocking chair on the other side of the chamber.

As he stood, he pulled the blanket with him and tucked it around his waist. The room spun. Worse, his legs barely withstood his weight. "Abed for two miserable days and I'm as weak as a bairn."

The lass glanced over her shoulder and blessed him with another smile. If a grin might give a man strength, Alice ought to keep at it. "I'm amazed to see you on your feet. After you spent the night moaning, I feared you'd never wake."

Quinn scratched the itchy stubble on his face. "'Tis not like me to moan."

"Everyone moans in the midst of a fever."

"I was fevered?"

"Aye, and sweating something awful. I couldn't replace the cloths on your forehead fast enough."

Deciding to forgo his shirt, he staggered to the bench and plopped on his arse, completely spent. "You mean to say you sat up with me all night, wiping my brow?"

When the young lady turned, her gaze dropped to his bare chest. Her teeth grazed her bottom lip. "And ladling willow bark tea between your lips. I'll say the reason you're faring so well this morn is on account of the tea." Dipping her head, her lips curved in a sheepish grin. "And a tot or two of watered whisky."

"Watered?" He grinned back, bless it he liked her. He especially liked it when she raked her eyes down his body. And by her expression, she liked him as well.

She placed two bowls on the table. "I didn't want to choke you."

"Not me. I was born swilling whisky."

"Is that what your ma told you?"

"Regrettably, I didn't really know my mother. She passed away when Eachan was born."

"I'm sorry." Sadness filled her eyes as she passed him a spoon—made of silver and embossed with a coat of arms. The piece didn't fit with the shabbiness of the cottage but before he mentioned it, Alice continued, "My ma passed the day I was born. I blamed myself for years."

"It wasn't your fault, lass. Childbearing has a way of taking too many young mothers from their bairns." He reached for the spoon and took a bite. "Mm. This is good."

"Thank you. 'Tis Gran's—"

"Recipe?" he asked. "I take it the woman has taught you a great deal."

"From herbs to facts to reading. She's a wise woman."

And odd.

A rose in full bloom sat in a crystal vase in the center of the table. "Is that the same bud you gave me?"

"It is." Alice cupped her hands around it and inhaled. "The fragrance is more potent than any rose I've ever smelled."

"'Tis not like any I've ever seen either. What sort of rose blooms violet?"

"A damask rose. Gran says they're...*special*."

Quinn's gaze traveled to the brooch he'd seen Alice wearing with the four emeralds. "How do you mean?" he asked, noticing the motto encircling a hand *Ne Parcas nec Spernas*. In his thoughts he translated the Latin, "*Neither Spare nor Despise*".

Alice ran her finger down the crystal vase. "I'm sure it is only myth."

"I've nowhere to go." He looked her in the eye. "Tell me."

"Och, if you must know, Gran says it makes enemies become—"

"What?"

She rolled her hand through the air. "Ye ken."

"Lovers?" he asked, praying it were true.

A glowing blush blossomed in Alice's silky cheeks. "That's what Gran says. She's not right about everything, though."

Chuckling, Quinn tapped the brooch. "But you just boasted about her wisdom."

Those lovely blues shifted toward the pin, but she uttered not a word.

"Tell me, bonny Alice, why were you at the high table wearing this?"

She stirred her pottage as if hesitant. "I'm the last of my clan."

"Which is?"

Though her blush deepened as red as hot coals, she squared her shoulders, tipped up her chin, and looked him straight in the eye. "Lamont."

Chapter Eight

As Alice clearly and proudly declared her clan name, the pain in Quinn's shoulder burned. Disbelief stifled his breath, as he gaped at the woman. Why in God's name had she taken him in? She'd stood over him with a razor-sharp knife. Why had she not run it across his throat?

"Lamont?" he asked, his voice hard as he raked his fingers through his hair. "Good Lord, woman, you held my life in the palm of your hands."

As she set down her spoon, the woman's gaze filled with a concoction of wild emotion. Anger. Defiance. And, most of all, pride. "Do not think that fact escaped me—not for one minute."

Quinn's mind raced. Damnation, why had she risked her life to help him? Why hadn't she let her kin finish him off in Rothesay?

The glint of the long sword by the door caught his eye. The lass could have finished him more than once. "And yet you tended me as if I were kin."

"Same as I would any living soul."

"But—"

Shaking her head, Alice held up a palm. "The day you rode onto my lands—"

"*Your* lands?"

"Aye, *my lands*!" She pounded a fist onto the table. "That day I raced back to Gran ready to poison the burn—to kill Argyll's grandson and heir."

His gut squeezed as he gulped. "But instead you brought me the rose."

"Gran's idea, mind you. But she..." Alice pushed back the bench and stood.

Quinn tried to follow, but when his knees buckled, he remained where he sat. "Go on..."

Alice busied herself with tending the fire. "Obviously she had different ideas. Which...which, were completely misguided."

"Hmm." Quinn again scratched his stubble as he studied the damned rose. The old woman might have had good intentions, but most likely for the wrong reasons. No matter if he wanted to court the lass, the odds were not in their favor. But the old woman needed to atone for her actions. Was the rose supposed to be a trick—some sort of medieval spell? Was the old seer indeed a witch?

He needed to think. He needed to breathe. And with the air in the wee cottage growing tenser by the moment, the only thing that made sense was to hasten outside. "Where might I find the well? I'm in need of a shave."

And a healthy dousing in cold water.

***

"Merciful fairies, I'm daft." Alice had collected a razor, soap and drying cloth for Quinn, but now that he'd gone outside with the blanket wrapped around his waist, he'd left his clothes still draped across the back of Gran's rocking chair. Surely he'd want to don his shirt and kilt after his he washed and shaved. Tiptoeing to the garments, she smoothed her fingers down the wool of her skirts. No, it hadn't escaped her notice that the Highlander appeared quite comfortable marching outdoors with her plaid hugging his hips.

Although, it wasn't as if Alice hadn't already seen his chest. She'd spent the past few days trying to cover him up, only to have the man shove the bedclothes back down in his fitful sleep.

Making up her mind, she collected the clothing and marched outside. At the corner of the cottage, the memory of the look in his eye when she'd told him her clan name made her stop. "Lord Quinn?" she called, clutching the clothing tighter. Was he angry?

When he didn't respond, visions, not of his fury, but of the man weakened by loss of blood, possibly collapsed in a heap and unconscious emboldened her. *I knew he was up and about too soon.*

But as she darted around the corner, the last thing she expected to see was...

Oh my.

Alice froze. She forgot to breathe.

Beautiful, pure, braw, and a very naked Highlander stood bent over a basin, ladling water atop his head. With a grand shake, Quinn straightened while he pushed his hair away from his face. Streams of water trickled down his body, making gooseflesh stand proud...his every muscle flex.

Too stunned to avert her gaze, Alice took it all in. Chestnut locks dripping onto shoulders powerful enough to pull a horse cart. From there rivulets of water streamed to a lean waist—lean but sturdy. She squeezed the bundle of clothing tighter as her gaze continued down Quinn's sculpted form. Aye, his buttocks were smoothly chiseled like marble—

but clearly not hewn of stone—hewn of dimpled, muscular, irresistible flesh.

Without noticing her presence, Quinn splashed under his arms, the sunlight making the water glisten as it trickled downward.

Alice's mouth went dry. If only she could touch him—trace her fingers over every defined muscle flexing beneath his skin. She took a step forward, a twig snapping beneath her toes.

Snatching the razor, he faced her in a crouch, eyes blazing.

Within a heartbeat, she took a step back. But she didn't avert her gaze, unflinching she couldn't help herself. He was long and sleek—potent and oh, so very male. Something deep inside filled with longing. Her breasts grew heavy, making the need to touch him grow tenfold. "Um..." Was he as delicious as he looked? Was the hair on his chest soft or coarse?

She managed to shift her stare to his face. "Oh my."

"Alice?" In the blink of an eye, his mien softened as he set the razor on the table and covered himself with the blanket. "You brought my things," he said, his voice soft and incredibly deep.

The tone alone made her tremble, excruciatingly aware of what she'd just seen—of every inch of his formidable body. Alice gulped and stared at Quinn's chest, heaving with his every breath. One of the roosters from the chicken yard crowed, serving as the slap she needed to remind her that this man was not someone with whom she could ever fall in love.

Clearing her throat, she held out the bundle. "Here you are."

After taking it, he set the clothes on the board and stepped nearer. "You've a fire coursing through your blood right now, haven't you, lass?"

Tough she trembled from head to toe, she couldn't force herself to turn and run. A fire coursing through her blood? It felt more like the sizzling coals made hotter by the smithy's bellows. "H-how did you know?"

"The same frenzied desire is thrumming through my veins as well." He slid his palm to her waist, long black eyelashes lowering while his gaze dipped to her mouth. "Tell me you don't want me to kiss you and I'll return to my bath."

Alice commanded herself to turn around and flee, but her legs refused to budge. Tingles raced across her skin. She couldn't breathe. The cock crowed again, and she barely heard it. Quinn's lips neared—beautifully full lips, slightly parted and looking like sin. As if it had a mind of its own, her hand grasped his waist—cool flesh, slightly damp. But his wee gasp made her melt like molten gold. "I—"

"Say it."

"Please." As she raised her chin, his mouth covered hers, gentle at first, but as she yielded, his lips turned hot, wet, insistent, rendering her powerless.

Something exploded inside her. This man personified the most forbidden fruit in all of Christendom, and Alice was coming undone in his arms. His kiss consumed her, uplifted her, made her ravenous. His soul poured into her like aged whisky until she was intoxicated with pleasure.

Digging her fingers into the bands of flesh she'd craved to touch only moments ago, she could not fight him.

Even if he is the enemy.

As if he'd heard her thoughts, he cupped her cheek and slowly drew away. "I ought not to have acted so brazenly. Forgive me."

Drawing her fists beneath her chin, Alice skittered backward What had they done? "This can never be."

"Unless..."

"Nay. As soon as you are well enough, you must go." She glanced out toward the sea, another worry twisting her heart.

"Gran should have returned by now. She might arrive at any moment."

"Are you certain?"

"Aye."

"Do ye ken what may have detained her?"

Alice shook her head. "I aim to return to Rothesay as soon as you're on your way."

"With the food and brisk bath, I've grown stronger already. I'm sure the fighting has been quelled. I'll escort you across the Clyde on the morrow. Besides, I must fetch my horse."

Chapter Nine

For the love of God, why hadn't he exercised some bloody control? What was it about Alice that turned him into a lovesick fool? She was a Lamont! Worse, whenever the woman came near, his mind blanked, his heart raced like hummingbird wings, and his bedamned cock turned into an iron rod.

She was the granddaughter of the man his grandfather had mercilessly put to death.. In her eyes, he had to be a complete and utter beast.

He must regain his strength *and* his senses and take control posthaste. Moreover, if he spent one more minute in the cottage surrounded by the scent of enticing, tempting, alluring Alice, he might make good on his reputation of scoundrel. And all because of her. She drove him mad with lust—the longing to put his hands on her body, to explore every inch of her flesh with his mouth. The hunger to be the first take her places she couldn't possibly imagine.

Damnation, the woman drove him mad, insane, and completely ravenous.

Heading for the Toward Castle ruins, Quinn spent the

remainder of the day forcing himself to rebuild his strength. He never should have kissed her. Heaven forbid, if she'd been naked he would have lost all control. Such an irresponsible act would have rekindled a clan feud, doubtless bringing Lamont allies from all corners of the Lowlands to put Campbell lands to fire and sword.

He considered strapping on his weapons and leaving, but he'd promised to help the lass find her grandmother. Bittersweet as his plan was, the idea of traveling with Alice and keeping her close tempted him beyond reason. On one hand, it might be nice to come to know her better—find out more about her—her likes, her loves, her plans for her future. But such musings were akin to the betrayal of his clan and kin. There could be no plausible future for them. A wee tryst would not be acceptable, either. Alice was too precious. She deserved better than to be ravished and cast aside. Worse, every time Quinn looked into her blaeberry eyes he yearned to kiss the lass. Hell, he wanted to do a great deal more than kiss.

If only she were a simple maid, a tryst might assuage his inexplicable lust. But no, the woman had to be a clan leader in her own right—the only living heir of the Lamont line. Of all the clans who feuded with the Campbells, Lamont was the most hated. Before the massacre, Alice's grandfather had led his kin on raids putting Campbell women and children under the knife. They'd reived Campbell cattle, burned out their crofts and attacked their castles, yet Quinn's grandfather had repaid their deeds tenfold.

By the time Quinn returned to the cottage, he was bone-weary, but a good fatigue, the kind that made a man feel as if he is on the mend after a bout of sickness. The sun shone like an immense yellow ball on the horizon of the western sky and, after a polite knock, he strode inside—a home far more meager than the lass deserved.

Alice set her mending aside and stood from the rocking chair, blushing scarlet. "I-I wasn't certain you'd return."

Was she embarrassed about catching him bathing? He hadn't given his nakedness a second thought, other than wishing they'd been naked together, other than wanting her more than he'd ever wanted a woman in his life.

He rubbed the back of his neck and let the door swing closed behind him. "I needed to regain my strength." *And clear my addled head.*

She'd brushed out her hair and the waves shimmered in the candlelight as she gestured with an upturned palm. "I made roast chicken."

"Is that what smells delicious?"

"Mm hmm." Feminine hips swayed while she moved to the hearth and tugged on the hob's cast iron handle. "If you'll open the bottle of wine, I'll set to serving."

Quinn found the squat flagon on the table and used his dirk to cut away the wax sealing the cork. "You look bonny this eve."

"Oh?" Placing the chicken on the table, she didn't seem to appreciate the compliment. "Not any different than usual, I suppose."

"Och, you'd look bonny dressed in sackcloth. The first time I laid eyes on you I thought ye were the loveliest creature I'd seen in all my days." He raked his fingers through his hair. *What am I about? Why must I become a lovelorn fool whenever I'm in her presence?*

A wee smile turned up the corners of her mouth. "A selkie."

"Nay, that's what my brother said. But I thought..."

She smoothed her hands down her apron. "Yes?"

"I thought you were as beautiful as a goddess."

His words produced not a smile or blush, but a coy

expression with wide, teasing eyes. "You've seen many goddesses, have you?"

"Dreamed of them quite a bit." Giving up on hiding his emotions, he grinned lopsidedly. "As it turns out I was dreaming of you."

Alice sat and nodded to the bench opposite. "Och, Lord Quinn, your banter is enchanting. If I'd not been born a Lamont, I might think you wanted to court me."

"Why should I not?" he said, barely believing such a question had slipped through his lips. "I enjoyed kissing you." *Mercy, can I not keep my mouth closed?*

The purse to her lips transformed into a grimace as she turned redder than a blood rose. Not meeting his gaze, she picked up a carving knife and pointed it across the table. "We must pretend that never happened." She set to chopping up the chicken as if it were tougher than leather.

Quinn leaned in. "Allow me, if you will."

Alice presented him with the knife's handle. "I never should have brought out your clothes."

Ah, so the incident out back *was* what had her bothered.

Quinn carefully sliced a juicy breast and set it on her plate. "It was very kind of you to do so."

"But weren't you..."

Ignoring the fluttering low in his gut, he focused on the task as he served himself. "Hmm?"

She scraped her teeth over her bottom lip. "*Embarrassed?*"

"Nay." He looked her in the eye but doing so peeled away a bit of the cool exterior he was trying to project. God Almighty, she was bonny—merely having her eyes upon him sent his heart aflutter. "I hope I didn't make you feel that way."

Alice suddenly became very interested in her food, pushing her chicken about the plate with her knife. "You're making me nervous now."

"Forgive me. 'Tis difficult *not* to look at you."

"Well, you must stop."

"Why? Because my grandfather was a backstabbing tyrant?"

Her eating knife stilled. "He killed my father and destroyed my clan—after my grandfather had surrendered."

"Aye, he did. Then he paid the price for his tyranny on the Grassmarket gallows."

The lass speared a morsel of chicken. "You have his blood coursing inside you."

Quinn slid his hand across the table and stopped right before he touched her fingers. "I am not my grandfather. Nor am I a tyrant. Furthermore, I do not and shall never condone his actions at Dunoon."

Alice said nothing as she ignored his hand and busied herself with pouring the wine.

Her silence may as well have been a dagger stabbing Quinn in the heart. "I wish I could go back in time and convince him of his follies."

"But you cannot." She picked up her glass and sipped, those beguiling blues watching him. Aye, Miss Lamont was quite good at hiding her emotions, though her eyes betrayed the pain lurking in her heart.

Quinn shoved his plate aside. "I thought all the Lamonts were..."

"Dead?" Her whisper came like a breath of frost.

"Aye." He took a long drink, wishing he had something more potent. Perhaps she was right. After his shave, he should have taken his gear and left. Without his mount he mightn't have made it all the way to Inveraray, but he would have had a good start. If only Alice's grandmother had returned, he would be free to go on his way.

Was that what he wanted? Hell, it certainly was what he

needed. He'd never see Alice again—leave her to return to her duties and he to his.

Then why did the thought of turning his back make the pain in his shoulder ache all the more? Did he not have a contented life before he'd met Alice?

"Most were killed," She continued, "some escaped to the Lowlands."

"But not you?"

"Gran hid me. She says I am the clan's last hope."

"And you have every reason to hate me."

"But I do not." Alice dabbed her lips with a linen cloth. "Why did you kiss me?"

Because you have bewitched me mind, body and soul.

"I couldn't help myself." Unable to sit without touching her, Quinn moved around the table and grasped her hand. "I want to kiss you again."

But this time he must exercise utter control. Out by the well he'd acted roguishly, taking her in his arms and plundering her mouth as if she was an alehouse wench. He didn't want to ever disrespect her. Alice deserved to be worshipped, loved, respected. Her entire clan had been wronged by his kin. If only he could find a way to help her—to make up for the sins committed four and twenty years ago.

Quinn moistened his lips and bowed over her hand, hovering for a moment. The soft fragrance of roast and rosemary mixed with the same delicious scent of woman he'd breathed in when he'd kissed her. Closing his eyes, his entire body ached to have her, to come to know ever inch of her flesh. To learn her deepest desires, her greatest fears. But if he never performed another chivalrous act in his life, he would control himself in this moment. The warmth of her hand caressed his lips as he gently kissed.

Alice's sharp inhale made Quinn's heartbeat stutter. On the outside he didn't show the intensity of his desire. Rather, he drew her knuckles to his cheek and brushed them along his face. "I am and shall always be at your service, m'lady."

"H-how do you manage it?"

His eyebrow quirked. "I beg your pardon?"

"Every time you look at me or touch me, you make my insides turn molten." She tugged her hand from his grasp and wiped the back of it on her skirts. "You have no right to seduce me."

"I didn't mean to…" Quinn groaned and shoved his fingers through his hair. "I meant to show you respect."

"By kissing my hand?"

"Aye, that's what courters are expected to do."

"Courters?"

Bloody hell, the more he said, the deeper he dug his grave. Quinn couldn't propose marriage to a Lamont. His father would crucify him.

Alice thrust her finger toward the pallet. "You have had a long day and quite obviously need rest else your shoulder will never heal. And do not expect me to stay up for nights on end spooning a tincture into your mouth. I simply will not do it."

Bowing, he nearly chuckled at her bravado. Was she fighting the same internal battle as he? *Most likely*. "I'm feeling much stronger now than I did this morn."

Shifting her gaze away, she twirled a lock of her hair around her finger. "T-t-that's quite good because as I recall, your knees were rather wobbly."

"Alice."

"Aye?"

"I want to kiss you again."

She raised her palms in front of her face. "Absolutely not. We cannot ever do that again. As you just so aptly demonstrated, merely kissing my hand is *dangerous*."

"You're right." A heavy weight settled upon his shoulders while Quinn strode toward his pallet, putting the table between them—not much of a barrier, but it would have to serve to remind him of his place. "'Tis a good thing we are setting out on the morrow."

"I ought to go alone."

He chopped his hand through the air. "Absolutely not."

"I beg your pardon, next you'll be telling me you forbid it."

"I doubt you'd listen if I did." Quinn started back around the table but clenched his fists and forced himself to stop. "It is not safe for a woman to venture out alone. What if you fell victim to outlaws?"

"Aye, as if you'd be much good to me with your injured shoulder."

Quinn rolled the offending wing, willing himself not to wince at the pain. "'Tis coming good. By the morrow I'll be swinging my sword with either hand."

"I doubt that. Not even a Campbell heals so quickly." She stood taller. "I can care for myself—have been all my days."

He shifted his fists to his hips. "Can you now?"

With an indignant spark in her eye, the saucy lass raised her chin. "Aye."

"You sound quite self-assured."

"I keep a dagger up my sleeve."

"A dagger?" Unable to resist, Quinn sauntered around the table. "What else?"

"I-I'm a fast runner. You saw it for yourself in the wood."

"Hmm." He eyed her from head to toe, approaching like a wildcat. Damn the bloody table. Quinn needed no weapons to make his point. As soon as he was near enough, he snatched her wrist and spun her around, putting her back against his chest.

He grunted. Stars shot through his vision. Jesu, his shoulder burned like a bastard.

"No!" she shouted, trying to stomp on his instep, but even through the pain, he was faster.

Quinn used his good arm to restrain her while he fished inside her sleeve and found the knife. "Is this your defense against vile miscreants like me?"

Her body tensed. "I told you where I hid it. The outcome would have been different had I surprised you."

"Many a woman conceals such a weapon in her sleeve or her garters." He tossed the dagger onto the table. "But a wee knife is no match for a dirk, musket, sword, or any manner of weapons."

She raised her chin, twisting enough to meet his gaze. "So, what would you have me do, strap a pistol to my waist?"

Good God, she personified temptation. Pert lips, the soft curves of her bottom flush against his loins. "I would have you allow me to accompany you on your quest to find your grandmother," he growled, his voice rasping. "Let me prove to you that I am not my grandfather."

She studied him, her gaze sliding to his mouth. Did she want to kiss him as much as he craved to taste her, just once more? Quinn dipped his chin a fraction. As if pulled by a magnetic force, she stretched nearer.

"How can I trust you?" she whispered.

If he kissed her now, he might lose what little trust he'd earned. "I give you my word."

"That's what your grandfather said to mine—afore he ordered the executions."

Jesu.

Quinn released his grasp and snatched the dagger from the table. "Then I give you leave to drive this blade into my heart."

Taking it, Alice turned the weapon over in her hand as if considering. "Nay, I believe what you said. You are not your grandfather."

"I am not, nor will I ever be."

"Then you shall carry out my bidding when we set out on the morrow. And we will not hide our identities. You are a Campbell aiding a Lamont in her search for her grandmother."

"And you are a Lamont accepting the assistance of a Campbell." He held out the palm of his uninjured arm. "Agreed?"

Her eyes narrowed as she stood proudly as if assuming the role of clan leader. And then she did something completely unexpected. The bold lass slit open her palm without so much as a flinch. "Hold your hand steady."

Quinn did as asked and she cut him as minimally as she'd cut herself. Seizing his palm, she pressed the two wounds together. "We seal this pact with our blood. Should either of us faulter, the other will put him—"

Quinn clenched his fingers tightly to prove his commitment. "Or her."

"Under the knife."

"You have my oath."

"We leave at dawn."

With a nod, she turned on her heel and dashed into the rear chamber, closing the door behind.

Chapter Ten

Alice watched Quinn drop a crown in the ferryman's palm in payment for their passage to the Isle of Bute. She had misgivings about traveling with a wounded man and suspected he'd opted to take the ferry because rowing the skiff would hurt his shoulder and he was too proud to accept her help.

Ferry or skiff, Alice didn't care. It was neigh time to find Gran. And the longer the dear woman was away, the more Alice feared something calamitous had happened.

I never should have left her.

"You oughtn't be taking a lass to the isle," said the ferryman, slipping the coin into his sporran.

Three men had already boarded. They were MacGregors by the look of them and armed to the teeth.

"What's afoot?" asked Quinn.

"I reckon everyone in the Highlands except you knows. The Lamonts have staged a bloody siege."

Alice clapped a hand over her mouth to muffle her gasp. "No."

Quinn grasped her shoulder. "He's right. You should stay at the cottage."

"Did you not hear him? The *Lamonts* are responsible for the rising." *Gran is with them. I should have known!*

"All the more reason for you to remain safely beside home's hearth," Quinn persisted.

"Is she sailing or nay?" asked the ferryman. "The others are waiting, m'lord. I must weigh anchor."

Without assistance, Alice boarded the boat. "I answer for myself and I sail."

The ferryman released the rope. "Have it as you like, miss, but His Lordship is right. Bute is no place for a lassie at the moment. Especially one as young and bonny as you."

Quinn pulled her aside. "Are you certain?"

Alice nodded. "The last time I saw Gran, she was embroiled in the midst of the skirmish. And now I ken my clan is at the heart of it, I must find her."

A grim smile twisted the corners of his lips. "Your granny seems like the type of woman who'd be leading the siege."

"Mayhap she is, though I'll not assume anything until I see it for myself."

Alice strode past the Highlanders and stood at the bow while the boat got underway. Was Gran at the center of the siege? Had she been responsible for Quinn's wound? What about the daft rose and what significance had it played? And who were the Lamonts holding the fortress? Over the course of her life, she'd met but a handful of her clansmen.

Before the boat arrived at the pier, a commotion stirred on the shore with men running and shouting.

Quinn stepped in beside her. "Those are my men. Stay close to me."

"I aim to put an end to this madness."

"And how do you expect to do that? Don a suit of armor and reenact Joan of Arc?"

"If I must."

"No doubt you'd do so without a flinch." He gave her arm a squeeze. "I hope it doesn't come to something so rash. But remember no one on the pier kens who you are. I'll be able to ensure your protection if it remains as such."

Alice pursed her lips. She had no intention of concealing her identity any longer than necessary. Gran had hidden her in the cottage for too many years. What was to become of the Lamonts who remained? She looked out over the sea of Campbells and their supporters. With such small numbers, her clansmen behind the curtain walls had little chance of holding the fortress for long.

A kilted man rode an enormous horse onto the pier—Glenn MacGregor—one of Quinn's companions. "Damnation, ye are alive, m'lord. I see you've brought along some reinforcements as well."

Quinn gave the man a snort. "Thought you'd take a holiday, in my absence, did you? With your girth I would have expected you to have the situation in hand by now."

"We've been busy enough. By my calculations there are no more than forty men holding Rothesay, though they have the ground advantage."

Quinn gave Alice a sideways glance. "We'll end this as peaceably as possible."

"Not one death," she said through gritted teeth. "On either side."

The corner of Quinn's mouth twitched up as he bowed his head. "M'lady."

"I am no one's lady."

He mumbled something that made Alice's stomach leap. Or was the sudden onslaught of butterflies caused by the rocking of the boat? Regardless of what she thought she'd heard, Alice chose to ignore him.

As soon as the ferryman set the gangway in place, she

followed His Lordship across while he strode straight toward MacGregor. "I need a complete run through of the present state of affairs."

MacGregor dismounted and handed his reins to a lad. "A moment first. I saw you hit by musket fire. Thought the worst. What the blazes happened?" He gave Alice a wary once-over. "Is she a witch? A selkie as Eachan said?"

Dissenting grumbles rose from the crowd. And by the way they were closing in, Alice said nothing.

"Stop with your misplaced suspicions. If it weren't for the lass, I would have taken another musket ball or worse. She saved my life. Tended my sickbed and brought me back to health in but a few days."

Quinn delivered a convincing argument, but Alice had seen his winces and heard his grunts. No matter what the man said, he was still hurting.

MacGregor frowned. "We thought they'd taken you behind the walls—which is why we haven't attacked."

"Good. No one attacks unless there is no other alternative."

"Let's smoke them out," said a ruddy Campbell.

His Lordship jammed his fists onto his hips. "I'd prefer to parley first."

"Are you daft?" MacGregor drew his dirk and thrust it toward the castle. "Have you lost your memory whilst you've been in fairy land? Those bleeding bastards tried to murder you."

Alice shoved Quinn far enough aside to push into the conversation. "I'll talk to them."

"No." His Lordship sliced his hand through the air, nearly hitting her midriff. "I cannot allow it."

She batted his hand away. "You are not my clan chief and I owe you no fealty. I will speak to them and there's nay a thing you or your behemoth MacGregor can do about it."

The big man scowled. "We can tie her up and lock the lassie in the stables."

"Shut it, Glenn," Quinn planted his feet wide and fisted his hips—a stance oozing complete authority. "I want everyone to ken right here and now, Miss Alice is not to be trifled with. She saved my life and for that we will treat her with respect."

He leaned to her ear and whispered, "If anyone goes in to parley, it will be me."

Before she could pose an argument, Quinn eyed his man. "Now, where's my brother?"

"He rode for reinforcements...and cannons."

"Cannons?" His Lordship asked.

MacGregor spread his palms to his sides. "We thought the bastards had you inside."

Quinn started up the hill toward a cluster of tents. "When do you expect Eachan to return?"

"No later than the morrow. This afternoon if we're fortunate."

"Do you have my weapons?"

"Aye, they're still in the tent, m'lord."

Hanging on every word, Alice followed closely behind. As soon as the top of the keep came into view, she searched the crenels for Gran—or anyone she might recognize. Merciful Father, if the Campbells were planning to bring in cannons, her clansmen would have no chance.

Chapter Eleven

Quinn sat at a table in the rear of the alehouse with Alice at his side and the wall at his back where he'd be able to act quickly and protect her if anything went awry. "Have they made any demands?"

Across, MacGregor nursed a pint of ale. "Not a bloody word."

"That makes no sense at all. What have they been doing for the past four days, having a *ceilidh*?"

"Same as us. The bastards—"

"Watch your language in the presence of a lady," Quinn growled.

The big man shrank a bit, looking like a chided mastiff. "Beg your pardon, miss." But Glenn quickly regained the classic MacGregor scowl. "We have ladders enough to scale the walls as soon as the cannons arrive. And thus far they've done naught but wait and watch. One of our musketeers fires off a shot, and they shoot back."

"Anyone injured?"

"Only you."

"They could have killed us all at the gathering."

Using her thumb, Alice squashed the candle wax pooling in the center of the table. "But they didn't."

Quinn drank his ale down and pushed the empty tankard toward his friend. "Go fetch us another round, would you?"

"Fetch your own bloody round." MacGregor might be full of brawn, but he carried a chip on his shoulder the size of Bass Rock.

"M'lord," Quinn added to emphasize their difference in station. He wasn't about to bend to his friend's irritability. "I need a word with Miss Alice."

"He's none too happy," she muttered after Glenn gave her a dark, disapproving glance and strode away.

"I wouldn't be either."

She drove her thumbnail beneath the wax, levering it from the wood. "And he's itching for the cannons to arrive."

Quinn rested his palm on his sword, something he did when he was about to step in harm's way. "That's why I'm going inside afore they do."

"Then I am as well."

"Absolutely not." He pulled her hand away from the candle and firmly placed it in her lap. "I forbid it."

The lass shoved her chair away from the table, her eyes filled with spite and gall. "For-bid?" she asked, drawing out the word as if it were blasphemous.

"'Tis too dangerous." Quinn slapped his palm on the table. Mayhap he'd overstepped his bounds, but he would not back down on this. "If I go inside under the flag of parley, they'll ken I'm willing to listen to their grievances."

"Flag of parley? I doubt *my* kin will trust you."

"They'll trust a man with no weapons. 'Tis the way of honor." He removed his sword and dirk and clanked them across the board. "Now tell me true, is your grandmother involved?"

73

"Gran saved you. I do not see how she could be aside from trying to prevent more bloodshed."

"But she was holding a musket when I was shot."

"And then she protected you—safeguarded us both."

"That's what perplexes me. Why would she do such a thing? Your grandmother is the wife of..." He swiped a hand over his mouth. "Ye ken. She has more cause to hate me than anyone in all of Scotland."

Alice levered up another glob of wax. "I'll tell you true, I've thought a great deal about her motives since she spirited us out of the castle, and I cannot make sense of it either. But I ken in my heart if Gran had wanted to see you dead, her musket would have had a smoke coming from its barrel and you would be in a shallow grave." Alice grasped his arm and squeezed. "I must go inside with you."

MacGregor returned with three tankards frothing over. Quinn held up his palm, requesting silence. He couldn't let the lass inside until he knew for certain she'd be safe. "Let me enter first. Once I understand their purpose, I'll send for you."

She pursed her lips. "I do not like it."

The big Highlander set the ale on the table. "What do you not like, miss?"

Quinn wrapped his fingers around a handle. "I've decided to walk across the drawbridge of Rothesay Castle alone."

"That hairbrained idea again? Have you lost your bleeding mind?" MacGregor planted his beefy hands on the table and leaned in. "They've already shot you once."

After taking a long drink, Quinn licked the foam from his lips. "I've made up my mind and nary a soul can change it."

HIGHLAND KNIGHT OF DREAMS

Once he crossed the bridge alone, the Lamont guards took their time searching Quinn for weapons.

"I reckon we ought to tie his hands," said one—a skinny whelp who looked as if lifting a Highland sword would be an effort.

Quinn held up his palms. "I came across carrying the black flag of parley. Even a Lamont would honor such a request to talk."

"He's right," said another.

"Aye?" The lanky one sauntered too near and inclined his lips toward Quinn's ear. "Not to worry. We'll have so many muskets ready to fire, if you make one errant move, we'll fill ye full of lead."

Quinn's shoulder throbbed, reminding him exactly how it felt to be shot. Still, even with his injury, he could strangle the maggot for his insolence. It would be easy to grab the dirk dangling from the man's belt and plunge it into his belly while using his body to block an attack from the other lout.

Quinn splayed his fingers. "I'm not here to fight. But if the time comes for battle, I'll nay forget your pimpled face."

The coward raised his fist. "I ought to—"

"Save your ire," barked the more reasonable of the two. "Come."

They led Quinn to the center of the circular courtyard. He expected to meet their leader, or Alice's grandmother, or at least someone who was waiting to talk. But he was met by two-dozen musketeers training their muskets on him from around the perimeter of the courtyard. For the better part of an hour he stood alone and, by the minute, he grew more certain of his impending death. At last with the screech of medieval hinges, a man wearing a mismatched plaid jacket and kilt marched from the tower like he owned the castle. Shaggy, obviously having gone without a shave for the duration of the siege, the black-haired varlet was flanked by twelve men, six on each side. Evidently, they weren't taking any chances.

"I'm Rory Lamont," he said, his voice gruff.

Looking the man in the eye, Quinn gave a nod. "I assume ye ken my name."

"So, the heir has come for a polite conversation, has he?"

Quinn glanced beyond him. "Where's the old woman?"

"She's lost her nerve."

"I need to see her."

"Why?" asked Rory. "She's naught but a female."

"She's the wife of James Lamont. If anyone has a bone to pick with me, it is she."

The man clamped his hand atop the pommel of his sword. "I have enough grievances for the lot of us."

"I'll oblige you and listen once I see the woman is unharmed."

"Oh, for the love of God, Rory, he's right!" Alice's grandmother hastened from the keep, her wrists bound, a gag around her neck.

The shaggy Highlander frowned. "Fergus, I thought I told you to keep her quiet."

In the doorway, a guard spread his palms and shrugged. "You watch over her next time."

Rory gestured to Alice's grandmother with his thumb. "So, you see for yourself Lady Lamont is well. I demand you return the lands stolen from the Lamonts after your kin backstabbed us at Dunoon."

The woman's title caught him unaware for a moment, but it was right. Her husband had been a knight. Presently, titles made no difference. Quinn took note of his odds—not good if things grew bloody. "Apologies, but my father possesses the deed, not I. He has not granted me leave to negotiate on his behalf."

The man smirked. "Then we'll hold you hostage until the earl arrives."

"You would take a chance on inciting my father's ire?"

"I don't give a fig about your father."

"And he mightn't give a fig about me," said Quinn, planting the seed of doubt.

"You lie. All Campbells are liars."

Rory motioned to his guardsmen. "Seize him!"

Quinn ran to the far wall. Using it as a barrier, he turned and threw a fist into the first guard's jaw while reaching for the man's dirk. Just as his fingers brushed the hilt, a vicious strike came from behind, jarring his wounded shoulder. Bellowing in pain, he spun to face his attacker. A wooden pole slammed across his neck, dropping him to his knees.

Two men held Quinn's arms while a third wrapped a rope around his wrists.

"Stop this!" Alice shouted, marching in from the hidden gate—blast—their only escape route revealed.

How the hell did she escape from MacGregor?

Chapter Twelve

❦

"There is another way," said Gran, pushing Rory and the guards aside.

The Lamont man scowled and stepped beside her. "I think—"

"You have bungled this enough." Gran pulled Alice in front of Quinn. "I'd hoped the rose would have—"

"Cease this nonsense about the rose!" Alice shouted. It was not up to her grandmother to lead their kin. And if she didn't act now, all would be lost...again. Taking charge, she threw up her hands and turned full circle, commanding the attention of every being in the courtyard. "I am Alice MacDonald Lamont, granddaughter of the slain James Henry Lamont. I am your clan chief and you *will* obey me."

She took another turn, slower this time, eyeing every man. "Lord Quinn entered these walls in good faith and we would be as underhanded as the Campbells themselves if we do not honor his request."

Gran took a step toward her. "But—"

"Nay!" Alice stopped her with a determined stare.

"Hear my supplication, Alice, chieftain of the Lamonts!" Gran shouted so loudly the courtyard turned eerily quiet.

Alice gave a nod. "Since you have recognized my authority, you may speak."

"Where is the rose?"

For the love of God, why was the silly rose so important? Alice stamped her foot. "You ask about a flower when our kin have broken the protection of parley?"

"Is it still alive?"

"Aye," Quinn said, rising to his feet. "It grows more beautiful by the day."

Gran hobbled forward and removed his bounds. "More beautiful than my granddaughter?"

Alice gripped the woman by the shoulder. "You are speaking nonsense."

"I will answer." Rubbing his wrists, Quinn took Alice by the hand. "Nothing of this earth can ever surpass the kindness and beauty of Miss Lamont. She is bonny within and without. She may not think she possesses magic, but she has bewitched my heart and it belongs to this woman and only this woman."

To the sound of her grandmother's gasp, tingles spread throughout Alice's entire body as she stared into the kindest, most loving eyes she'd ever beheld. "Truly?"

Quinn squeezed her hands. "Truly."

Gran's sigh echoed between the walls. "The rose blooms to turn enemies…"

"Into lovers," Quinn finished. He grinned as wide as the sea. "I do not believe in the power of the rose, but I do believe in the Lamont leader standing before me."

"In the name of the Earl of Argyll, throw down your arms!" a shout bellowed from the wall-walk.

At least a hundred Campbell men stood elbow to elbow, ready for battle.

Boom!

A cannon fired. The entire castle shook.

"Stand down!" Quinn ordered. "I have committed to a peaceable resolution."

"Without consulting me first?" Archibald Campbell sauntered into the courtyard, wearing a courtier's periwig and a bold plaid. "You might be my first-born son, Quinn, but I am still earl."

"You are, but there are circumstances to which you should be aware."

"Oh? Pray tell afore I order the execution of these miscreants."

Quinn licked his lips, his gaze flickering between Alice and his father. "I have a question I will ask first."

The earl gave a nod, though he looked her from head to toe with distrust in his glare.

But Quinn remained undaunted. Keeping one of her hands between his palms, he kneeled. Alice moved to pull him to his feet but stopped when he grinned. "Alice MacDonald Lamont, you have brought me back from the brink of death. You have shown me kindness when you had every right to hate. Before God and our clans, I ask you. I beg you. To be my wife."

Gasping, a myriad of emotions swelled in her breast—bewilderment, a wee bit of fear, surprise and finally joy. Suddenly it all made sense, Gran's rose, sending her to him in the dead of night, and helping them escape at the fête. Her eyes brimmed with tears as she smiled and nodded. "'Tis right for us to marry." And by the warmth spreading through her entire body, she knew for her entire life she had been fated to wed this man.

Standing, Quinn faced his father. "I have chosen my bride, the future Countess of Argyll."

The earl clutched his hand atop his chest, looking as if

he'd taken an arrow to the heart. "A Lamont?"

Quinn tightened his grip on her hand. "My Grandfather —*your* father wronged these people. All they want is to return to their rightful lands."

"My lands." Argyll pointed his finger. "You cannot give away that which is not yours."

"Perhaps, but the only wedding gift I ask for is the lands of Dunoon. If you grant me this one thing, I will see to it the fishing industry is restored and the crofts pay our coffers tenfold what they earn now."

By the narrowing of his eyes, the earl was actually considering Quinn's proposal. "And how do you plan to guarantee this turn of fortune?"

"If I do not return these profits within five-year's time, I forfeit my title, but Dunoon will remain in the hands of the Lamont clan."

"Hmm." The earl paced for a moment before he met his son's gaze. "This is not the alliance I would have wished for you to make, but given you are willing to put so much on the line, I agree to your terms."

As shouts of joy rang around the courtyard, Alice pulled Quinn into an alcove. "Are you certain about this?"

"I am."

"But we barely know each other."

"Does it matter?"

"Did you propose merely to avoid bloodshed?"

"That was a secondary reason. And I ken my father. He would fight to the death to keep Dunoon in the family. Our marriage serves two purposes."

"To unite Lamont and Campbell forever."

"Aye, but there is something more important."

Alice's tingles returned tenfold as she smiled, encouraging him to continue.

"I'm in love with you."

"Truly?"

Quinn cupped her cheeks and kissed her mouth like a man who knew exactly what he wanted. "I meant every word I said. I love you and I want you to be mine with every fiber of my being."

Sliding her fingers to his waist, Alice drank him in, reading the love in his eyes. And in that moment, she knew she would never want to be parted from this braw Highlander in all her days. "I love you, too." Throwing her head back, she laughed. "How did it happen so quickly?"

He surrounded her in an embrace and filled her with warmth. "I think it may have had to do with a damask rose and something about wisdom and the reversal of a curse."

Alice slipped her fingers around his waist and met his gaze while happiness thrummed through her veins. "Nay, 'twas no curse that came between our kin. 'Twas the hate between two men who took a clan feud too far."

"And together we will mend our differences and our children will grow stronger, their hearts beating with the blood of Campbell and Lamont." Quinn dipped his chin, his dark eyelashes shuttering his chestnut eyes as he captured her mouth in a slow, claiming kiss. A kiss powerful enough to douse the fires of hell. A kiss that would end hatred in their corner of the Highlands once and for all.

Also by Amy Jarecki

Highland Defender
The Valiant Highlander
The Fearless Highlander
The Highlander's Iron Will

Highland Force:
Captured by the Pirate Laird
The Highland Henchman
Beauty and the Barbarian
Return of the Highland Laird

Guardian of Scotland
Rise of a Legend
In the Kingdom's Name
The Time Traveler's Christmas

Highland Dynasty
Knight in Highland Armor
A Highland Knight's Desire
A Highland Knight to Remember
Highland Knight of Rapture
Highland Knight of Dreams

Devilish Dukes
The Duke's Fallen Angel
The Duke's Untamed Desire

ICE

Hunt for Evil

Body Shot

Mach One

Celtic Fire

Rescued by the Celtic Warrior

Deceived by the Celtic Spy

Lords of the Highlands series:

The Highland Duke

The Highland Commander

The Highland Guardian

The Highland Chieftain

The Highland Renegade

The Highland Earl

The Highland Rogue

The Highland Laird

The Chihuahua Affair

Virtue: A Cruise Dancer Romance

Boy Man Chief

About the Author

A descendant of an ancient Lowland clan, Amy adores Scotland. Though she now resides in southwest Utah, she received her MBA from Heriot-Watt University in Edinburgh. Winning multiple writing awards, she found her niche in the genre of Scottish historical romance. Amy loves hearing from her readers and can be contacted through her website at www.amyjarecki.com. Visit her web site & sign up to receive newsletter updates of new releases and giveaways exclusive to newsletter followers.

Printed in Great Britain
by Amazon